FIC MC
Monter
Captai
R0021

D0099207

DEC - - 2005

# Captain of the Sleepers

# Captain of the

# Sleepers

## MAYRA MONTERO

Translated by Edith Grossman

Farrar, Straus and Giroux

New York

Farrar, Straus and Giroux
19 Union Square West, New York 10003

Copyright © 2002 by Mayra Montero
Translation copyright © 2005 by Edith Grossman
All rights reserved
Distributed in Canada by Douglas & McIntyre Ltd.
Printed in the United States of America
Originally published in 2002 by Tusquets Editores, Spain, as *El capitán
de los dormidos*
Published in the United States by Farrar, Straus and Giroux
First American edition, 2005

Grateful acknowledgment is made to Luce López-Baralt, for use of her
translation into Spanish of some verses from "Moradas de los Corazones"
by Abu-l-Hasan al-Nuri of Baghdad.

Library of Congress Cataloging-in-Publication Data
Montero, Mayra, 1952–
[Capitán de los dormidos. English]
Captain of the sleepers / Mayra Montero ; translated from the Spanish by
Edith Grossman.
p.   cm.
ISBN-13: 978-0-374-11882-2
ISBN-10: 0-374-11882-5 (hardcover : alk. paper)
I. Grossman, Edith, 1936– II. Title.

PQ7440.M56C3713 2005
863'.64—dc22
                                                                2005040056

Designed by Jonathan D. Lippincott

www.fsgbooks.com

1   3   5   7   9   10   8   6   4   2

*For Susan Bergholz and Beatriz de Moura*

*And to the memory of two men:*
*Vidal Santiago and Roberto Acevedo*

R0021129152

It never happened, never.
It seemed to—so oblique, so fine,
so damp and dark . . .
It seemed to, perhaps, because
for a moment our mouths were filled with dirt
as if we were the dead.

                    —From the Spanish, by
                    Dulce María Loinaz


The past is not dead;
it is not even past.
—William Faulkner

# Captain of the Sleepers

I'M in the last place on earth I'd like to be. Waiting for the last person in this life I thought I'd ever see again. It's almost six. I'm sipping beer at the bar of the Pink Fancy, a hotel on St. Croix where I arrived just a few minutes ago, carrying a small week-end bag.

When I arrived I was registered by a woman who didn't stop laughing. She was young and fairly heavy, and apparently she could not forget the joke that another employee—a man who was looking over some papers and laughing quietly too—had just told her. I asked about my reservation, and with a thin, high-pitched voice she answered in the kind of correct English that was unusual on this island. Then she handed me a brochure with a map of the city (she didn't give me time to explain that I could walk around Christiansted with my eyes closed), drew a circle around one of the restaurants, and recommended that I be sure to eat there. I agreed with a smile that I'm afraid she thought was mocking. She drew back, behaved like an offended butler, and told me drily that my room was on the second floor. Before I went up I asked her for Mr. Bunker's room number, John Timothy Bunker; I stressed each syllable and seemed to hear my father's voice: "J.T.," which he pronounced in English, not Spanish. That's what he always called the Captain of the Sleepers.

I went upstairs and took a deep breath before I picked up the phone. How long had it been since I'd heard his voice? Fifty years, fifty-one in a few months. The last time I talked to him I was twelve years old, standing in the entrance to my father's small hotel. In the midst of all that sorrow it was where I took refuge, and the Captain tousled my hair as he passed by; he usually did that. He took a few steps, and then he stopped to see if I'd say anything to him. But I didn't open my mouth, I went on shuffling the cards I'd been playing with, so he decided to speak even though his voice sounded different. He said: "It's how you grow up, son." I didn't understand the meaning of that sentence until many years later. By then, I'd begun to wonder if what I saw was really what I saw. And I'd also begun to wonder if it was really worth killing the Captain, which was what I'd sworn to do no matter where I found him.

The listless voice of a frail old man answered the phone. "This is Andrés," I said. "I'm here."

I didn't count on his beginning to sob. That was my first impression, and then I thought perhaps they weren't sobs. Maybe sitting up, picking up the phone, or simply speaking was a great effort for him. Especially speaking; he himself had told me that the cancer had reached his throat. He paused and murmured: "Thank you for coming." I didn't answer, and he went on to say that he'd arrived the day before from Maine and was exhausted, but we could meet in an hour at the bar. I assured him I'd be there. I had a hunch he was going to say something else, but I didn't give him the chance. I hung up; I was panting and had the feeling I'd been running for my life; yes, to save it, but for how long?

I turned on the TV, hung up my clothes—a jacket, a pair of trousers, the shirts Gladys had been folding as she told me not to go to St. Croix—and opened a bottle of water. Then I lay down on the bed, and as soon as my head touched the pillow I decided I had to move quickly. I took the key and walked out to the corridor. I went down to the bar and ordered a beer. I couldn't permit myself the luxury of just going down and finding the old man waiting for me. To begin with, I didn't want him to say that now I looked even more like my father, and when he saw me come in, with the light behind me, he imagined it was his friend Frank walking toward him. Though my father didn't live to see sixty, and I'm sixty-two. Sixty-two years that I don't carry very well; I'm sure I look older, which I don't care about one way or the other. I felt old, I got used to being old from the time I was a boy.

The Captain, by my estimate, must be eighty-three, too old for that uncomfortable flight from Maine, stopping in San Juan and changing planes for the Virgin Islands. But I must confess I wouldn't have agreed to see him anywhere but the Pink Fancy. Only here do I have the courage to face what he's going to tell me. Courage, and the kind of foreboding that lets you throw everything overboard. This hotel, almost as old as I am, tells me everything. I came here often as a child; I played here on vacation, and during those years it was my favorite place. In fact, I once asked my father if we could paint the windows and eaves of our little hotel on Vieques blue and change its name: instead of Frank's Guesthouse we could call it the Blue Fancy. But Papá refused, and now I find it logical that he wouldn't have wanted to. He told me to get my own hotel when I grew up and call it whatever I liked. I didn't do that. I studied law, and it never occurred to me to run a small hotel on the beach. I suspect it's too late now to try to open one.

"Too late," I repeat, and instinctively I look at my watch. I'm in the last place I want to be, it's six-fifteen, and I've finished my first beer. I'm getting ready to order the second when I see him coming toward me. How far can a man fall without collapsing completely? The Captain is wearing the kind of hat he always wore—a dark panama—very wide khaki trousers, and a white polo shirt that's too tight and mercilessly reveals his sharp-pointed bones. He looks everywhere except at me, though for the moment I'm the only person sitting at one of the little tables in the deserted bar. Not for an instant does he attempt to look at me, though he recognizes me, of course. He recognizes the boy he stopped seeing but has always seen. A nightmare recurs and torments him, a terrible one in which he sees my eyes, I'm sure about that. If not, he wouldn't have done anything to meet me here.

I stand and hold out my hand. He does the same, and as we shake hands I detect the stink of vomit. The smell comes from his clothes, perhaps from his skin; I suppose he was vomiting just before he came down to see me. By the time we sit down, I'm better able to confront his ruination. That's the word to describe his face, which has been distorted in the worst possible way: a lizard's eyes in violet-colored sockets, devastated ears like those of a leper, sunken cheeks tinged with gray.

"This is what cancer's like," he says with a smile, as if he'd guessed what I was thinking.

I wonder how he sees me. Fifty years have gone by and I can't declare a victory. Not much of that suntanned twelve-year-old boy, with his curly hair and cleft chin, could be recognized in this pale, flabby, totally bald old man. A mortar shell in Vietnam almost tore off my leg. They managed to save it, but I walk with a limp. When it's going to rain, I limp and feel pain and a kind of rage that makes me tighten my lips involuntarily; the rest of the time I barely notice my limp.

"Do you shave your head?" the Captain asks.

"Hardly at all," I reply. "There's not much to shave up there."

He starts to laugh, and again it's as if he were sobbing.

"I'm not feeling very well," he confesses. "I finished a cycle of chemotherapy three days ago."

"You already know why I've come," I say, unmoved. "I don't want you to feel worse."

The Captain shakes his head. The waitress comes over and

asks what we'd like to drink. He orders whiskey in a brandy snifter. I ask for another beer.

"I'm almost as old as you," I say, trying to maintain a neutral, almost mild tone. "I could have died years ago, when I was in Vietnam, or last year, when I collapsed in the middle of the street; I came out of that with a pacemaker. Take a look at me, J.T. Don't you think I have a right to know what happened?"

I could swear the Captain looks at me joyfully. He tightens the line of his mouth, where there are no longer lips or anything that resembles them. Though I'm seeing them in my mind. I see his mouth, his lips full and well-defined beneath his slim mustache, and his determined jaw, the classic jaw of a fearless redhead. Which is what the Captain was.

"Ask whatever you like," he says defiantly, raising his voice and narrowing his eyes, as if he suddenly could not bear the humble light of the world. It's begun to grow dark.

"Just tell me if you did it."

"Yes, I did something." He spits out the words slowly, like seeds that he's been sucking. "I won't be sorry when I'm dead."

He says *dead*, and I recall the word *death* on his lips. "You don't talk about death." That's what he said to me the first time I got into his plane, a Parakeet Cessna (my mother gave it that name because it was green and blue). As soon as I knew I was flying and looked down at the beach—the beach, and the gray spot my father had turned into—I asked him if we were going to fall. He didn't answer, and I repeated the question in a louder voice, using different words: I asked him if we were going to die. He stopped laughing and concentrated on the sky: "In my plane you don't talk about those things. You don't talk about death." I must have been about seven, and my father, who had insisted on my flying with the Captain, came with us to Roca Escondida, the beach next to the small, improvised Mosquito landing strip used by only two pilots: Reverend Vincent in his silver de Havilland, and the Captain of the Sleepers in his

Cessna 140. Papá used to say that those of us who lived on the
islands had to get used to flying from the time we were children.
On that occasion, my mother agreed with him. She buttoned
my shirt and suggested I pay attention because I was going to see
the spread from the sky. She gave the name "spread" to the pair-
ing of the small hotel and our own house, an old wooden build-
ing in the back that in those days seemed to me like a mansion
too big to be encompassed, with three or four rooms on the second floor, and a basement where Papá kept the old beds that he
replaced in the hotel.

"How long since you've been to Martineau?"

The Captain's voice, which is not entirely his voice, tears me
from my daydream as if I were being torn from an enchanted
womb. The strip of beach in front of the hotel, the hill behind
the house, the small hollow with the dry woods, all of that land
was called Martineau.

"I haven't been there for decades. I have no reason to go."

"Of course you have a reason," he protests, with a touch of
irony. "But you can't force things. One day, you'll suddenly feel
like seeing how it's changed. I've heard they've built another hotel in Martineau, in the same spot. You're going to feel like confronting all that."

"I only want to confront one thing," I say, biting off each
syllable.

The Captain shudders but goes on talking. He says that a
year ago, when he learned about his illness, he felt the impulse
to see me again, the impulse to return to Vieques. He called his
friends on St. Croix, the few he had left, and found out I lived
in San Juan. After that it was fairly easy to get my telephone
number from an operator, and even easier to call the house and
ask my wife if I was in.

"Your wife," he exclaims, as if he just remembered, "didn't
she come with you?"

"She didn't want to," I tell him. "She didn't want me to come either."

He moves his head, controls the impulse to ask why.

"I talked to her," I explain in any event. "We were married thirty-two years ago, but we've known each other for forty. There isn't much she doesn't know about me. She knows about this."

He raises his left hand, leaves it in the air for a moment, and then suddenly lowers it onto my hand. I feel as if it were the involuntary movement of a skeleton that somebody had shaken after centuries of immobility.

"It never happened," he says, trembling. "Not in the way you imagine."

I look at my glass because I'm afraid I have no beer left. There's a silence, which the Captain uses to take up again the thread he has let drop, the sibylline point of the story. He composes himself and murmurs that he's happy to be back on St. Croix, especially in the Pink Fancy. Here, this hotel, is where he came hundreds of times in the company of my father, starting in the days when it was a private club for the sugar barons. This same bar is where they drank and talked about matters of interest, exchanged confidences, and perhaps felt mutual envy.

"I miss Frank." His voice comes out in a falsetto. "I always missed him. And the food at the hotel, he had a good cook there, that Elodio, imagine my remembering his name. Not to mention Braulia, who cooked even better."

He orders another whiskey, and I ask if the doctors allow him to drink. He replies that in his condition they allow him almost everything. We fall silent and continue drinking. Not moving. Waiting. Finally he orders his third drink, and when they bring it he lifts his hand again but doesn't let it fall on mine; instead, he raises it to his throat and pinches the scaly skin under his chin with two fingers.

"I can explain what you saw."

I feel a mouthful of beer slowly overflow my stomach and begin to rise to my chest. When I was twelve, after I saw the image of the Captain for the last time, I had the same sensation but with a different liquid, perhaps bile, perhaps blood. That night I began vomiting and was still vomiting the next morning, and the day after that, and on each successive day. I couldn't tolerate anything in my stomach, and my eyes were becoming sunken. They moved me to San Juan, to a hospital where they gave me shots. I turned into a half-crazed boy, staring at the wall and talking to imaginary lights. It took more than three months for me to recover, and when I went back to Vieques everybody thought they'd put another boy in my place.

"That day," the Captain whispered, "I tried to crash the plane into the reefs at La Esperanza, but I didn't have the courage. When I got to your house, I already knew I didn't have the courage." He pauses and slowly drains the last swallow from his glass. The liquor trickles from the corners of his mouth. "My head was on fire . . . my lungs hurt, I was soaked. Don't you remember that I came to your house dripping wet?"

No, I didn't remember. In my memory, for all these years I'd seen him dry. Dry and abject, like a dark piece of wood.

"I wanted to stop and talk to you," the Captain mutters. "But I had to keep going. I needed someone to comfort me." He passes his hand over his mouth, the back of his hand. It is a menacing gesture, and at the same time a defeated one. "Then I did what I did. That comforted me."

# CHAPTER ONE

CHRISTMAS Eve of 1949 was the last one we spent together. And I often think the corpse of that man was a sign. There was a corpse in the house with us that night: the remains of a desperate man who took his own life on St. Croix, but before that he'd asked to be buried on Vieques.

By then I knew that the dead were dead: people who would never wake up. But there was a time, when I was four or five years old, when they had me believe that the corpses transported by the Captain in his small plane were travelers who had fallen asleep.

When I was that age my father would take me to the Mosquito landing strip to pick up cases of provisions or liquor, and cases of bed linen or towels that he'd ordered for the hotel. If the Captain happened to have a dead person with him—someone who had died on Isla Grande (Big Island is what we called Puerto Rico) or on St. Croix, someone whose family felt like spending the money to bury the body on Vieques—he sat it down beside him, like a copilot, and covered it with sheets. My father would find some excuse to take me aside and tell me in a quiet voice: "He's sleeping. The Captain's going to wake him now."

It wouldn't have mattered to me very much if they'd told me it was a corpse. I didn't have a very clear idea of death, and I'm sure I wouldn't have tried to find out anything else. Except once, when one of the bodies, a pregnant girl who died of tuberculosis,

suffered a mishap when they arrived. The Captain went to take the
girl out of the plane and hand her over to her parents (who'd been
waiting for their dear departed just like we'd been waiting for the
case of provisions), and the flowered sheet covering her became
soaked with blood. We were all deeply affected because the body
also gave off a cloying, repugnant smell. It was a troubling smell
that penetrated my bones. My father covered my eyes and said,
"Don't watch her sleeping." The Captain's hands were stained, and
later I saw him wiping them with a rag. The girl's parents, who'd
brought a coffin with them, put her in it without pulling back the
sheet and left, not saying goodbye, in the same one-horse wagon
they'd arrived in.

John Timothy Bunker, who devoted himself to carrying
freight in his Parakeet Cessna, was born in Maine, but when he
was fifteen his father took him to live in the Virgin Islands. The
old man, Lawrence Bunker, an engineer and combat pilot, had
been one of the group of advisers who recommended the ac-
quisition of St. Croix to President Wilson. J.T. liked to say that
on the day he was born, his father couldn't be in Port Clyde
with his wife, who was giving birth for the first time, because he
was in Christiansted throwing out the last of the Danes. Years
later, old man Bunker got sick of the Caribbean and wanted to
return to his roots: the secret fishing on Monhegan Island and
the red sunsets of Muscongus Bay. His son chose to stay on St.
Croix, earning a living with his small plane, transporting cargo
or passengers, whichever paid more. In 1941, a reporter from
New York who was writing an article in Christiansted asked J.T.
to take him to Vieques. They both stayed at Frank's Guesthouse,
my father's little hotel. I was two years old at the time, and my
mother, who must have been twenty, posed with me for the reporter near the cliffs of Puerto Diablo. The photograph appeared in *The New York Times*, and behind my mother, who held
me in her skirt, you could see the silhouette of a large battleship.

The caption under the photograph said that President Roosevelt and Admiral Leahy were traveling on the ship.

After that first trip, J.T. became my father's friend and began to make frequent flights to Vieques; every two or three months at first, and then, in '43 or '44, when he arranged to be a subcontractor for a man who in turn held contracts with the Navy, not a week went by that he didn't come to the island and, in passing, to the hotel, taking advantage of the opportunity to bring something my father had asked for, and at times a toy for me too. In general, he carried food and electrical equipment. Occasionally, if he had room, he agreed to carry a passenger or two. In those days, a good number of people who had lost lands and livestock in the expropriations being carried out by the Navy (we almost always used the English word, *Navy*) were moving to St. Croix to look for work. Some were unlucky enough to die, and of all those who did die, barely a handful could allow themselves the luxury of returning to the cemetery in Isabel Segunda. That was true of the corpse we sheltered on Christmas Eve 1949, a tormented soul who, without intending to, added more fear to our fear, and more anguish than we perhaps could bear.

Papá was shaving when my mother sent me to tell him that John (she never called him J.T., or Captain, or any other name but that one) needed to talk to him. Sometimes, when he brought in a corpse on the plane, its muscles and bones became so rigid he couldn't move it. Then he'd ask some boy idling on the beach for help, someone strong enough to straighten out the bones of death, and hungry enough or poor enough not to feel either disgust or fear.

But that afternoon J.T. didn't find anyone near the Mosquito landing strip who could help him. The dead man's family had not come at the agreed-upon time to pick up the body. By now the corpse was as stiff as two stuck dogs—that was the description my father used—and its arms and legs so contracted it was

almost impossible to get the body out of the plane. The Captain
came to our house, holding his dark panama in his hands, turning it round and round as if he were looking for a sign in the
hat, and in a quiet voice he told my mother what had happened.
He was sorry to bother us on a holiday, but he needed the help of
his friend Frank. My mother drew herself erect; she would always
stand erect in a way that, over time, began to seem contradictory
to me: she would thrust out her chest and look straight ahead, like
a pigeon about to impose its authority, which was not very natural in a woman with a character as peaceful as hers. Standing erect
in that way, she told the Captain that a dead person is a dead person and could not spend the night outdoors. I was a few steps
away from my mother and heard everything, thinking it looked
like a disagreement but knowing it really wasn't. She asked me to
find my father, who as I've said, was in the bathroom shaving.
Papá went out with traces of lather on his face to get the keys to
his truck, since the Captain was driving his Willys, a military vehicle we all called Eugene the Jeep, where nobody would have
dared to seat a corpse. They sped away, and my mother put her
arm around my shoulders but didn't say anything.

A couple of hours later, when it was getting dark, they came
back. They were crestfallen and spoke to my mother in whispers. She turned and looked at me, and I pretended to read the
comics in the newspaper. I heard her say: "Andrés, come with
me to the kitchen." I stood up and followed her. She gave me
some of the sweet she was preparing as our Christmas Eve
dessert: it was a custard with tears. My mother called the drops
of lemon juice she squeezed over it "tears," and they were slow
as they ran down the sides of the custard, slow and tremulous,
as if something were hurting the dessert.

We sat down at the kitchen door that opened onto the
courtyard, the courtyard that in turn led to the service door of
the hotel. She watched me eat the custard, and when I happened
to look up, I suddenly discovered a bitter sight: my mother, who

three or four months before had looked just like the actress in *Buffalo Bill*, who was certainly the same one who'd been in *The Mark of Zorro* and was not called Pretty—Linda, Linda Darnell—for nothing, didn't look like anybody anymore, not like that actress, not like herself. At least on that day, in the weak light that faintly lit the kitchen, my mother had dark circles under her eyes and had been transformed into something delicate but unknown. She began to talk to me, and I didn't listen; I was trying to examine her face to find out what had changed.

"Do you hear me, Andrés?" She knew I was paying no attention to her, but I nodded that I was. She persisted: "Listen to me just for a minute."

Only then did I hear her talking about compassion, about the dignity of the dead, about what was for me even more incomprehensible: the flight of the soul, which was a silent spiral and the sleeper's true repose. In short, the corpse of the man who'd hung himself on St. Croix, and whose family my mother thought she knew by sight because everybody knew everybody else on Vieques, would spend the night in our house, and my father and she (she, at least) would watch over him until dawn. She added that at my age, in addition to numbers and verbs, I had to learn about the cruel blows in life. John (she said John, and it was as if she were speaking about a different man, not the Captain or J.T., who were the same person) had gone with my father to Isabel Segunda to look for the family of the unfortunate man. But they hadn't found anyone, not even a distant relative, willing to take charge of him.

My mouth was dry. Perhaps I turned a little pale. My mother must have thought I was shaken by the fact that a dead man would spend the night with us. But I hadn't even stopped to think about that. My dry mouth was due to her mouth—livid, as if it were bloodless—and my fearful eyes were due to her eyes, which no longer were like Linda Darnell's, and weren't even pretty, though they were still very mysterious and intensely deep. She preserved that knowledge until the end.

While she was talking to me, my father and the Captain took the body out of the truck and put it in one of the rooms. The hotel housekeeper, whose name was Braulia and who was my mother's right hand, helped the men with preparations. Before supper, Mamá let me go up to see him. They'd laid him out—to me, at least, he didn't look like two stuck dogs—and crossed his hands over his chest; they'd placed flowers around him, and his fingers held a rosary. On her own, Braulia had sent for four large candles and placed one on each night table and two at the foot of the bed. A sheet covered him to the waist. I approached and saw the mark of the rope on his neck. Then my mother told me to wash my hands. I said I hadn't touched him, and she, somewhat surprised, murmured that it wasn't because of the deceased but because we were going to have supper.

The Captain was invited to share our supper with us. As I recall, he'd never been there on Christmas Eve. He'd come instead on Christmas Day, with a present for each of us: he'd bring perfume for my mother, and on one occasion he brought her some records of songs in English. He'd bring my father a bottle of liquor, or cigars. And he always brought me an airplane, for Christmas he'd give me one of those planes you had to put together piece by piece, using glue. I already had five of them, and five was all I got. In 1949 he didn't give me one.

My mother and Braulia served supper. And when we were about to sit down at the table, Mamá said she missed her sister and her sister's family, her husband and children, who for the first time in many Christmases had not been willing to make the trip from San Juan. She said this in a quiet voice, not adding another word, because we all knew that the Navy had forbidden launch traffic between the Port of Mosquito and the Port of Ensenada Honda, and for that reason the crossing from one island to the other took twice as long. My cousins would get seasick, it was too long to be throwing up your guts on the rough December ocean, and nobody completely trusted the old launches they used back then. We remained silent, and Mamá caressed the embroidered flowers on the tablecloth, which was the most elegant one we had and was hardly ever used the rest of the year. She did this with a gesture of ancient weariness and murmured that in the end they'd take us off Vieques, they'd move everybody, like animals being transferred from one pen to another, and give us a pittance for our house and the hotel. My father swallowed hard and said it would be better to change the subject.

"It would be better to talk about the dead man," I suggested.

It came out just like that, a sentence that now might seem very heartless or very adult, but in the middle of that somber conversation, it was like a consolation. The Captain began to laugh and looked at my mother, who pressed her lips together because she was still upset. Papá poured me some liquor, just a drop to wet my lips. Mamá prayed quietly, and we all waited. Then she held out her glass and tapped it gently against mine. We toasted and said *"Feliz Navidad,"* except the Captain, who raised his glass and said "Merry Christmas." Then he looked into my mother's eyes, and she whispered: "Merry Christmas, John."

We finished supper, and I didn't start to play right away, as I did at other times. At that age it's impossible to distinguish between what is concern and fear, and what is exhaustion or the doglike need to save oneself. A glance was enough for my mother to decide that I was collapsing with fatigue. She walked over to me, her hands damp from washing the dishes, and put one of her enormously cold hands on my forehead. "Go to bed, Andrés." I looked up and stared at her lips, and even today, after so many years, I'm convinced her lips were whispering "Merry Christmas, Merry Christmas." They continued moving, as if repeating a visceral psalm, the inner incantation that marked her breathing.

I stood up, and instead of going to my room I went straight to the balcony where J.T. and my father were smoking in silence, but they'd said something that was still floating in the air. Something that in some way was crushing them and in passing hit me in the chest, as if I'd been struck by the tail of an invisible fish. My father, at least, seemed pressed into his chair. And J.T., sitting on the railing, made a strange gesture, stretching his neck and moving his head from side to side. They looked at me without seeing me, and I went back to the dining room. Suddenly, the presence of the dead man became a reality for me, and I realized I didn't want to go up to my room alone. My mother was still drying dishes. Her lips were quiet now, they didn't seem to be whispering "Merry Christmas" anymore, and maybe for that reason, because she was herself again, she paid more attention to my face and saw that I was afraid.

"I'll go up with you," she said, smiling without really wanting to.

We went up, and she waited with me while I brushed my teeth. Then she tucked me in and asked me to say an Our Father, "even if it's just one," for the dead man in the next room. I promised her I would, and she began to take off her apron, as if she were going out or were about to receive a visitor. She assured me she wouldn't leave the man's side for the whole night because she'd be praying for him, keeping a vigil the way you were supposed to. I was sorry my mother was going to waste her time at the foot of a stranger's bed, but at the same time I was comforted by the idea that the dead man couldn't get up or come into my room in search of warmth or company. My mother, awake next to that corpse, was the best guarantee he wasn't a sleeper. Somebody who at any time could cough, sit up, or vomit blood. It was the sleepers I was afraid of. I found that out before I closed my eyes. And confirmed it before dawn on Christmas Day 1949, which was silent and torrid. An endlessly hot day.

# CHAPTER TWO

THE dead man's family came the next morning to pick up the body. The sound of voices woke me. I went to the window and saw that they were taking him out on a stretcher, completely covered by the same sheet. My father and J.T. were helping them. Two old people, who must have been the dead man's parents, and a young man, who might have been his brother, took our stony Christmas Eve guest away in a noisy, open truck that raised a large cloud of dust as it drove off. I looked at the dust and was afraid the house would not be the same again. As if the corpse had taken with him our former life, or the instrument for getting back to it: a tiny key in his contracted hand.

It had been a long night for my mother. And in another, impenetrable way, it was a long night for my father too. I knew this as soon as I looked at his face. Christmas was the only day of the year when Papá woke me, and almost the only one when I saw him in pajamas. The rest of the time he ate breakfast at five in the morning, and when my mother called me, at about seven, Papá had already left for La Esperanza to buy fish or had gone to the port to pick up a guest. That morning he came into my room in his dark green pajamas. He came in thinking about something else but was surprised to find me standing at the window. He tried to smile, in a certain sense he succeeded, and wearing that wan, cold smile he kept looking at me. A lock of hair fell over his forehead, and his cheeks and mustache were wet. A few drops of

water ran down his chin onto his chest, and he was slowly rubbing his hands. It's the image of him that has always stayed with
me: Papá's recently washed face and the desolate fury rising to
the surface of that face. He realized I'd been awake for some time
and had seen everything through the window.

"Now he'll rest," he said, referring to the deceased, as if the
unfortunate man had also spent a miserable night.

My mother was waiting for me downstairs, next to the little
tree surrounded by gifts. She was wearing a flowered dress I'd
never seen, following her custom of wearing new clothes for
the first time on Christmas Day. It seemed to me she'd gone
back to being Linda Darnell in the movies, become Linda Darnell again in her character and her illusion of being happy, and
for a few hours that illusion could erase the devastation on her
face. She made a gesture inviting me to take my presents: one
from her, the other from my father. My father's was a baseball
mitt, and hers was a Zorro costume. In addition to the hat and
mask, which she had ordered from San Juan, she'd sewn a black
cape and shirt that she put in a separate box. I didn't ask for J.T.'s
present; I didn't ask with my mouth but I did with my eyes, in
a very subtle understanding between my mother and me: the
Captain hadn't left a present for me. From then on, after I'd put
on my Zorro costume, I can evoke only moments of the rest of
the day, like fragments of a dream in which I see my mother
frightened and my father taciturn, a thread of agony trembling
between them for the entire morning. When it was time for
lunch, I wanted to wear my mask to the table. I do remember
that, because Mamá reprimanded me, but she did it in a very
gentle voice, and my father tried to come to my defense, though
now I think he was only defending himself. He shouted—
almost shouted, he never really shouted—that for just one day,
just for once, on a Christmas Day that, after all, we were spending by ourselves, there was no reason to stand on ceremony. As
my mother listened to him she looked away and stared at a cor-

ner of the floor, while he kept looking at her; I saw them both through the gloom caused by the mask, a color that was like a presentiment.

In contrast to my mother, Papá had dark skin and straight, very black hair that he insisted on combing back, straight back without a part, though he couldn't always keep it there. His father had been a Lebanese merchant, a traveling salesman who sold costume jewelry and came to Vieques every two or three months, and on one of those trips he became involved with his best customer, a woman several years his senior who owned a boardinghouse in Isabel Segunda. Papá was the fruit of their relationship. He was born when his mother was almost forty, and he saw his father—who recognized him as his son and gave him his name, the same Yasín that's my name too—only two or three times in his life; when the Lebanese died, soon after his fiftieth birthday, he left my father all the money he had saved, which was enough to start another business. Apolonia, my grandmother, closed her boardinghouse in Isabel Segunda and bought the mansion in Martineau that she converted into a small hotel. She named it after her son, Frank, who was fifteen or sixteen at the time. We kept the original sign for a long time; a hurricane blew it down, but we kept the pieces.

Mamá's origins were much more genteel. She'd been born on Vieques, but her parents and an older sister had come to the island from San Juan toward the end of 1914. Her father, who was an engineer, was hired to build a bridge (a bridge that later became shrouded in a black legend), and encouraged by the contracts that kept coming his way, he decided to stay and build the house in Isabel Segunda where my mother was born. I had no memory at all of my maternal grandmother, because she died in 1942. But the image of my grandfather, who died several years later, was still fresh in my memory: a robust, pale old man who always despised the marriage of his younger daughter to the illegitimate son of a wandering Lebanese. My grandfather died as the result of a fall, when he was trying to climb into one of the sloops he owned. In his old age he'd taken to acquiring schooners and sloops that he used to transport merchandise around the islands. It had fallen to J.T. to carry the corpse to Christiansted, since my grandfather had asked to be buried there. At first, when they read his will, no one could understand his desire to be buried on St. Croix. Then it was discovered that on St. Croix he had another wife and child, a boy somewhat older than I was, as dark-skinned as his mother, to whom he left all his boats. My grandfather left a fleet to his little black son.

I'm certain my mother thought about all that in the final days of December. We took food and clothing to the dispossessed, who at that time were living crowded into camps the Navy set up for them in the Montesanto district. At first they'd been given a little money, and every week there were deliveries of canned food and cornmeal, as well as charcoal to cook on. But as the months passed, the deliveries became less frequent and the dispossessed became aware of their bones. My mother and Braulia, sometimes accompanied by the gardener, would bring them extra food, and the bed linen and most of the worn towels my father couldn't set out for the guests. As we were making our way to the camps on one of those afternoons, my mother remarked that even one of the schooners that had belonged to my grandfather certainly would have come in handy. "We could make good use of it now. Your father would have hired a skipper to sail it around the islands, to sell merchandise. That brings in money."

She was dreaming out loud; I realized she wasn't exactly talking to me, much less to Braulia, who was always a few steps ahead of us because she was in the habit of walking very quickly. She was talking to herself in a serious voice filled with resentment. The only thing she inherited from my grandfather was the house in Isabel Segunda, which by now was fairly rundown. For some time the neighbors had complained about hearing and seeing the old man's ghost, limping near the mastic tree in the courtyard. In life he hadn't been lame, but they attributed the limp to his fall from the sloop. That was why a good deal of time went by before anyone showed interest in renting the house. This was a tailor from St. Thomas, who installed his shop on the ground floor and outfitted an apartment upstairs for himself and his family. The man sewed trousers and jackets for the Marines and often repaired their clothing. He was punctual with the rent, which was not too high because nobody paid much for any house in Isabel Segunda, a town that was falling apart and at times smelled almost as bad as Montesanto. And I say almost because, as far as stinks were concerned, Montesanto outdid anything that anybody could imagine. During the dry months, the reek of dead animals was unbearable, and early in May, when the first rains fell, the stench of human shit and piss, mixed together, would rise into the air. Braulia, who was very clean and tidy, would soak a handkerchief in cologne and hold it to her nose. She did not remove it even to speak, since she spoke very little, almost not at all to the poor people living behind the fences under the canopies made of twigs, getting wet when it rained too hard, and broiling during the hot months.

"This is to make things more bearable," my mother would whisper as she distributed little bags with biscuits and candies for the children, and sometimes herring, the least expensive dried fish. Braulia walked in front, always in front, with bundles of clothing: shirts too small for me and worn trousers donated by my father, as well as a skirt and blouse given by my mother, which for her were like a promise; both articles were still "in fine shape" (that was Braulia's expression), ironed and folded in a separate bundle. They were given to a woman who'd recently given birth. Although women died occasionally, the ones who'd just given birth died like flies, and then they'd be buried in that clothing, which was by far the best they'd ever owned. We didn't know this right away. Braulia found out about it somehow, and in February or March, when Holy Week was approaching and my mother again began collecting clothes for the dispossessed, Braulia stood with her hands on her hips and exclaimed: "Do you remember the blue blouse we gave away last Christmas?" My mother said she did, and I, who was listening to the conversation, tried in vain to remember what the blouse looked like. "It's falling to pieces in the cemetery, Doña Estela, that's where it's rotting."

Estela was my mother's name, but Braulia as well as the rest of the staff—the cook Elodio Brito, the two girls who cleaned, and the gardener, whose name was Gerónimo—added the Doña out of respect. My father called her Estela, plain and simple. And the Captain called her Stella, not pronouncing the *E*, and he in turn was John for my mother.

Three or four days after Christmas we went to Montesanto for the last time. From there, instead of returning home, my mother, who was driving Papá's truck, decided to go to Isabel Segunda to pick up some presents my aunt had sent from San Juan. Mamá gave Braulia money to buy washbasins that were needed at the hotel, as well as plates to replace the ones that had been chipped or broken. My mother and I went to pick up the presents. We came to a house where we'd never been before; she knocked at the door, and we waited a few minutes, uncomfortable because we were in the sun. A short woman named Antonia opened the door, and this Antonia, who greeted Mamá very warmly, insisted she come in and stay awhile. She looked at me with some hesitation. I didn't ask, but Mamá gave me permission to cross the square and pass the time nearby; better yet, I could go to the store and see if Braulia needed help. It may seem strange, but I decided to find Braulia. I didn't care about carrying packages for her; what interested me was the shop, a kind of general hardware store that had postcards and chewing gum, lengths of string for flying kites, and fishhooks of all sizes. I had twenty-five cents in my pocket. A fortune in those days.

I started walking, not hurrying. If I didn't see Braulia, so much the better. I had an excuse to stay awhile looking at the display case and then go to find her in the only place Braulia could be: the house of her sister Matilde, who lived in Isabel Segunda. It was the end of 1949, and there were Marines everywhere, a good number of soldiers recently arrived from Panama, some with girls from Isabel Segunda and others in groups, crowding into the cafés, laughing with guffaws that sounded like howls.

Braulia was in the store, but when she saw me she put on an irritated face and raised her hand to her chest. I wasted no time telling her that I hadn't run off, that my mother had stayed to talk with Antonia and had sent me to help her with the washbasins. Her irritated face didn't change, but she took her hand away from her chest and turned her back to me. For a few minutes I didn't know what to do. Braulia's enormous body—she wasn't fat, but as my father would say, she was big-boned—hid part of the display case. The rest of the store was a jumble of planks, tin plating, traps for linnets, kerosene lamps. When the clerk finished wrapping the basins in sheets of newspaper, which he did one at a time, Braulia paid and stood looking at me.

"Let's go," she said.

I lowered my head and dug in my heels in my corner, knowing I was defying her. For the past few months I'd been defying Braulia, a woman who'd been present at my birth and was in the habit of giving me more orders than my own mother. I replied that I was going to buy some marbles, and I said it so softly she couldn't hear me.

"You're going to buy what?"

"Marbles," I shouted, and the clerk looked up.

Braulia walked away but stopped at the door. "All right, when you finish go to Matilde's house. I want to see you there in half an hour."

Matilde, in addition to being Braulia's sister, did the laundry for the hotel. Once a week my father brought her bags of sheets and towels, and Matilde and her two daughters washed all the linen and returned it dry and folded in the same bags, which were stamped FRANK'S GUESTHOUSE. The dirty laundry was generally delivered to her on Mondays. My father would put it in the back of his truck, and after dropping me off at school he'd go to Matilde's house and give her a list of the pieces he was delivering: so many sheets, so many pillowcases, so many towels. Matilde, in the meantime, would pull the articles out of the bags, while her living room filled with the smell of other people's bodies. During vacations I liked going there with my father, and when I turned eleven it was my job to read aloud the list that came with the laundry so that Matilde would know what we were giving her. But she just kept pulling out the articles and shaking them, as if she didn't hear me, and that odor filled my nostrils, and I liked it or was disgusted by it depending on which guests had used the items.

A month earlier, however, all that changed. It was the day before *Acción de Gracias*, Thanksgiving to the Marines. I went with my father because there was no school, and for the first time Matilde asked him to pay her in advance. My father protested, but then he took out his money and started calculating the bill. I became bored and walked to the courtyard, to the place where the clotheslines were and where, in addition to the hotel's laundry, Matilde always dried the shirts and trousers of the men in the Navy, and their underwear, sparkling white in spite of everything because she and her daughters ruined their hands scrubbing so hard. Behind the lines was a shed where they kept the soap and bleach and some cloth balls that contained pieces of bluing. The shed had a door with holes in it that had been gnawed by mice, I suppose. I also thought the noise I heard was mice scratching at the wood. The eight o'clock sun was as strong as if it were noon. I approached the shed and heard the brief moans of a small animal. I looked inside and found that Santa, one of Matilde's daughters, was moving back and forth under another body, which I immediately knew was a Marine's because of the eagle tattoo on his shoulder. I couldn't move. I opened my mouth to breathe and stayed there watching them. Santa had wrapped her legs around the man's waist, and after a minute she partially opened her eyes, looked toward the door, and saw me there; she saw my idiot's face and trembling mouth but decided to ignore me.

I don't know how long it all lasted; the man began panting, and I thought my father must have finished settling accounts and would be looking for me. I walked away from the shed, crossed the courtyard, and went back to the living room, and then I understood that time had been eternal only for me, inside my own head, since it hadn't passed for either my father or Matilde. Papá was still counting out the money, and Matilde was fixing coffee. Neither of them had noticed my absence or realized I'd returned, and so I slipped out again and ran to the washtubs and hid just in time to see the Marine come out, stop for a moment to pull up the zipper on his trousers, then take a shortcut to the street. As soon as he was out of sight, I went to see Santa. She was sitting on a wooden crate, wiping her chest with a damp towel. She looked up when she heard me approach but then returned to what she was doing: she dipped the little towel into a bucket of water, then squeezed it out and passed it between her legs.

"Don't tell anybody," she said as she stood up.

It was the first time I'd seen a naked woman. And what most attracted my attention was the black line that ran from her navel to her sex. I took a couple of steps into the shed. Santa was cleaning her thighs, and I saw a dollar lying on the ground next to her wrinkled dress. That's when I felt the pressure of her fingers grasping my arm.

"I'll let you touch me," she proposed, "but don't tell anybody."

She pulled me to her, pushed my head between her breasts, which weren't large or small, just hot, burning briefly against my face. I didn't do anything. I didn't open my mouth and I didn't move. She took my hand and placed it between her thighs; at first I touched coarse hair, and then it was wetness that opened to my fingers. I withdrew my hand, pulled out of her embrace, and went back to my father, who when he saw me, said only "Let's go," and then he said goodbye to Matilde.

From then on, I insisted on going with him to drop off or pick up the laundry, and on three or four occasions he agreed to change the routine: first we'd go to Matilde's and then he'd take me to school. The first time, Santa was washing clothes with her sister; we looked at each other, and nothing happened. But another time, when we arrived very early, I found her alone in the courtyard, said hello to her, went into the shed, and a little later she came in too. She took off her dress and put her breasts in my face, kissed me where she could, on my forehead and my hair, grabbed my hand and pushed it again to her belly, lowered it a little and held on to it tight. I didn't move; she was the one who was moving against my fingers. That lasted a couple of minutes, and then she told me to leave because they could see us. I told my best friend, a boy in my class who was a year or two older than me, and he begged me to take him to see Santa right away, but that was difficult. Every time I went to her house I was with my father, and I couldn't bring anybody else along. Then he told me that next time I should take off my clothes too and climb on top of her, like the Marine had done. I promised I would, and at night I'd go to bed with that idea in my head, but I'd never dared to take off my shirt; the furthest I'd gone was to bite her breast gently, and I did that because Santa asked me to in a quiet voice; she moved my hand and was crying when she asked me to. Almost crying.

Suddenly, on that morning toward the end of December, Braulia, without knowing it, pronounced the magic words. The store and its showcase ceased to exist. For the first time, I'd go into Matilde's house alone; I could walk straight to the courtyard, like a person going to play with his marbles, without the shadow of my father waiting for me in the living room. I felt a tingling in my stomach. I left the store and spent some time walking aimlessly, avoiding the street where Matilde lived, to give Braulia time to get there. Then I couldn't stand it anymore and began to run. I saw Braulia still in the doorway, talking to Matilde and two other women. They all went into the house without having seen me, and then it occurred to me to take the shortcut into the courtyard, the same one where I'd seen the Marine slip away that day. The washtubs were empty, and I didn't find anybody in the shed, but I lay down on the ground and looked up at the roof for a while and imagined that everything my nose detected—the smell of bleach, of soap, of warm laundry at rest—was nothing but the smell of Santa.

I was ready to leave when I heard voices outside. I looked out and saw her talking to her sister, soaking laundry. Both of them looked at me; Santa gave a little cry and walked toward the shed, while the other girl stood there laughing. She came up to me and kissed me on the cheek and was about to take off her dress to do what we always did, but instead of embracing her and biting her breasts, I began to take off my shirt too. She looked at me in confusion and asked what it was that I wanted. I said I wanted to do the same thing the Marine did, to get on top of her. She agreed but wouldn't let me lower my trousers. She lay down first and called me to her. We did the same thing we'd done so often standing up: I rubbed my face against her breasts, and she guided my hand. But that morning I felt that everything was different: for the first time, the tingling in my stomach went down to my groin, and then it went back up again and exploded in my skull and made me sob, just like Santa was sobbing. And so when she relaxed and told me to get up and leave, I didn't want to go. She said it more emphatically and pushed me. "Get off, stupid. My aunt'll come."

I stood up in a daze, put on my shirt, and left without seeing Braulia or waiting for her. I went straight to the house of that woman, that Antonia, where I'd left my mother. The truck wasn't there anymore. The sun blinded me, and I banged on the door, very hard. I remember those blows as the first man's blows I ever gave in my life. No one opened, even though I was there for a long time, pounding constantly. Then I looked through one of the windows; the living room was empty, with no trace of my mother or the woman who lived there. I sat down on the curb and tried to impose some order on my mind. I hated to have to go back to Matilde's house to find Braulia. I suddenly hated Santa and her sister. And above all I hated my mother, who'd disappeared just when I needed her most, because I needed to get away.

I spent more than half an hour hating. Then I stood up and went back to the store. There was Braulia, in a rage, almost trembling, and she asked me where I'd gotten to and said she'd been looking for me for a long time. She harped on the fact that the streets were no longer safe for a boy of eleven. Too many fights, too much drinking, because it seemed as if the entire Navy had landed in Isabel Segunda. Besides, nobody could tell her that in that mob of soldiers there wasn't some pervert running loose.

"Do you know what a pervert is?"

I kept silent, and she said she'd talk to my father. Then she seemed to hesitate, not knowing where to go or what to do with me.

"Let's go find Doña Estela."

I told her my mother wasn't in her friend's house, and the truck wasn't there either. Braulia replied that we'd find her, that she must be looking for us too. She spoke in a hostile voice, very different from her usual querulous tone. She tried to take my hand, but I wasn't the right age or in the right mood to have anybody lead me around like a child. At my insistence we stopped to have cane juice at a street stand; we were both thirsty, and her neck was sweating. As we were drinking, I thought I saw a man in the distance wearing a hat and hurrying toward the port, and it seemed to me it was J.T. I wasn't certain it was him, but I said to Braulia: "There's the Captain."

She looked and shook her head. "Nobody's there."

Isabel Segunda was boiling, and some Marines had taken off their shirts. My mother didn't appear, but she was another blast of heat burning our backs in what was almost a betrayal, especially of Braulia, who looked dazed. I was dazed too, but in a different way. I had marbles in my pocket and an unsuitable smell on my fingers. I raised them constantly to my nose and wasn't even capable of looking up; I couldn't while I was breathing in that smell, Santa's smell. Braulia could; she walked around and scanned the horizon searching for some clue, some trace. On that day so filled with signs, the only invisible steps seemed to be those of my mother.

"Thank God!" Braulia sighed after a while. "Here comes Doña Estela."

We got into the truck in silence. Mamá gave no explanation that I can recall. I see all of this as if it were at the bottom of the sea, with a murky landscape and a murky ride home. Papá was waiting for us, somewhat alarmed by the delay, and he helped us unload the packages. While we were unwrapping the basins, he and I alone in the kitchen, he asked me if I'd had a good time. I shrugged, and he looked into my eyes. It was a strange glance of comprehension and searching. A small embrace in the solitude.

*I'M a man of few words. You must know that better than anyone. As a young man, I rarely worried about misunderstandings; things happened, sometimes they happened to me, and it never occurred to me to give any explanation. It wasn't pride, Andrés, but a lack of time, or of compassion for myself. In the end, I discovered there were fragments of my life— especially everything from that time in my life—that were left hanging, like little animals rotting in full view of everyone. This story rotted in the same way. Because I didn't take the trouble to write either. I should have written to you. I often thought about doing it, but in the long run I didn't know how to begin the letter. Most people, when they grow old, find out they've spent their lives giving explanations, and they're sorry about that. Just the opposite happened to me: it really bothers me that I was so be-grudging with mine. I took it for granted that each piece, each of those mysterious pieces of truth and lies, would fall into place on its own.*

*You've come here to pull a confession out of me. You think it will make you live better or die more peacefully. And yes, perhaps you're right, though you still have some time to go before you die. I don't have bad feelings toward you, even if you do brag about your pacemaker. You're a young man compared to me—you must be sixty-two, sixty-three at the most, I think I'm a little more than twenty years older than you—and you still have to cross the frontier of seventy, which is ago-nizing and an affliction. And so look around you, accept what I'm showing you: this little hotel that once united us and, just as you see it, with its stupid pink color, was a thousand times more important in my life—in our lives, I suppose—than everything that happened to us later.*

*We spent a good many nights here. I don't know if you can remember that. I brought everybody in the Cessna Parakeet, as your mother called it (I wrote "Little Parakeet" next to the tail), and your father would sit beside me. You and your mother were behind us, laughing every time I sang that song. I bet you don't remember, but you learned it by heart and sang it on New Year's Eve, the last day of 1949. We'd land at the old airport north of Frederiksted; afterward I came to miss it. The runway was narrow and fairly short, but it was very well designed, well positioned, and there were almost never any surprises. My friend William, who had a beat-up old Chevrolet, would pick us up sometimes and bring us here, to the Pink Fancy. You'd start to run along the cobblestone streets, because in those days Christiansted was almost the same Danish village my father had known in 1910. Estela would go to her room to rest, and I'd sit in this courtyard—who knows, maybe at this very table—having a drink with Frank.*

*Your father, like me, was the kind of man who didn't talk very much and didn't like giving explanations either. We told each other what was absolutely necessary, and that may be why we became such good friends. It surely was the reason he chose me, trusted me to transport the weapons. But you know this. He must have told you about it. He didn't care that I'd been born in Maine. On the contrary, nobody would suspect the son of a combat pilot. I traveled all the time, and people knew me very well; they saw me load and unload, leave and come back. Who could guess that on one of those flights I'd fill the Cessna with pistols and bullets, and later with the rifles and carbines used in October? October, Andrés, just think about it: in all these years there hasn't been a single October that hasn't tasted like shit to me.*

*The weapons came by sea to St. Croix, since the coasts of Puerto Rico were being watched. A guy in Monticello, Florida, sent them, I never found out who, a trafficker like any other. Your father's job was to wait for the cargo on St. Croix, in a fairly isolated spot that's still known as Butler Bay, to count the pieces in each crate, hide them among the packages for his hotel, and send them on quickly to Vieques. At first your father's friends planned to carry the weapons to La Esperanza in a rented schooner. But Frank warned them it was dangerous; he believed he had the man who could transport them in his plane. I was that man, and of course, the idea terrified the nationalists. Everybody trusted your father. But me? Who could trust a dissolute, half-crazy gringo who lived from hand to mouth transporting provisions, and sometimes corpses, in his small plane?*

*Your father began to sound me out. We had strange conversations right here, in this bar. I couldn't figure out what it was that he wanted to ask me, and I began to feel discouraged. Several times we came to St. Croix, just the two of us, and occasionally we went out with women. In those days we all did it. Right behind the men who came to Christiansted to make some money were the girls who also needed to earn a living. We went to bed with some of them but didn't bring them to the Pink Fancy; we took them to a much more modest hotel, the old Hibiscus, on the docks.*

*One night when we'd had more to drink than usual, I saw a woman I liked on the street and asked her to come with me. Then I asked your father what he planned to do, if he was going back to the hotel or was going to find somebody to take to bed too. It seems he was tired of beating around the bush. "I want you to carry some weapons for me in your plane," he blurted out. I shook my head and gave the woman a couple of dollars so she could go on ahead and rent a room. When we were alone, I took your father by the arm and asked him what weapons he was talking about, and what he needed them for, and what the hell was he getting involved in. He asked if we could talk the next day; he looked exhausted and I couldn't think of another thing, any other damn miserable thing but to say that if he liked the woman waiting for me at the Hibiscus, he could go instead of me and take her to bed, it was all the same to me. I did it to make him happy, to relieve the tension a little, but I realized right away I'd made a stupid mistake. Along with the exhaustion in his face, I thought I caught a glimpse of hatred.*

"I couldn't," he whispered, biting his lips. "Don't you see that she looks too much like Estela?"

And it was true. The woman bore an intense resemblance to your mother; she had the same wavy hair, between ash-colored and light brown, and the same way of pinning it back on one side with a barrette and letting it hang loose on the other. She had the same changeable green eyes—dark green like volcanic rock—the same brow, cheekbones, everything the same. I felt a strange fury and wanted to punch your father and punch myself for being an imbecile. I turned and staggered away. I don't remember if I went to meet the woman or if we went to bed. I swear I don't remember anything else that happened. Probably I kept on drinking and then went to find her, and by then she'd have left, tired of waiting for me. I erased that night many times. I erased it for a few days and then, when I least expected it, it would reappear and cause me grief. I couldn't understand then what was happening to me. Now I do understand; at my age everything seems very clear, so simple it hurts in my memory. Even you can understand it. Your father always knew me much better than I knew him. And your mother, who was pure intuition, knew both of us perfectly. Perhaps she guessed our thoughts, I don't know, but eventually she knew everything about me. We were a triangle, why deny it? Not the classic love triangle but a kind of imperfect, quivering figure whose outline sometimes disappeared against a background of secret shadows. It would depend on how much tension existed among us.

On the one hand there was you—unless she lost her mind, and in the end she did, your mother wouldn't have done anything without taking you into account—and on the other there were the nationalists, the coming revolt, the secrecy with which they had to act, to dissimulate in front of the guests. Your father began to behave with a coldness we'd never seen in him. And Estela turned to stone; it's incredible, but she wasn't afraid, not for herself and not for your father. I don't know if she was afraid for you, about what could happen to you if Frank were arrested and she was, too, for aiding and abetting all of them. We never talked about death, about the absolute possibility of dying. We did talk *about prison, but not about being shot. As for me, I wasn't very convinced about what I was doing or why I was doing it. But I became involved because your mother was a challenge to me; she was so committed, risking everything. On the other hand—I'm dying, Andrés, I don't intend to hold back a single word—I confess I became involved out of jealousy. Not of your father, of course, that would have been ridiculous, but of the other one, listen to his name, do the impossible and remember his face: I'm referring to Roberto. He'd just gotten out of prison in Atlanta and was still gaunt after his years behind bars. He was very tall and good-looking, but not very talkative, more the kind of hard, obsessed man compared to whom your father and I must have seemed like two phantoms, two little piles of manure. I'm sure that if your mother backed them and ran the same risks they did, to a large extent it was because of him. They'd known each other since they were children; they'd grown up together in Isabel Segunda and had written to each other for years. I didn't know this right away, I found out later, toward the end, when she gave me some letters to throw into the ocean. Can you imagine, Andrés? Do you understand now why I went crazy? And yet I know what you think: there's no madness that can justify what you saw, or what you thought you saw. No, nothing justifies it because it didn't happen.*

*The first weapons arrived along with a corpse. I'll bet it was the first dead man you'd seen up close, knowing he was dead. Because at first, so you wouldn't be afraid, your father told you that the dead people I transported in my plane had fallen asleep. You already called me Captain, and that completed my nickname: Captain of the Sleepers. That was really a deep sleep. Swell carrion, sometimes the smell made me dizzy, that stink spread and clung to my hair and clothes. In 1949, on Christmas Eve, I brought to Vieques the corpse of a man nobody knew and nobody was waiting for. I did it in case the police intercepted me in Mosquito. They never had, but it was enough that I was carrying crates of weapons for the first time for my bad luck to give them the idea of searching me, and if they searched me, it would be impossible to justify transporting pistols.*

*A corpse was something else. Being taciturn, and declaring that I was carrying a poor soul who had died of tuberculosis, was a solid alibi. Not many people felt an urge to take off the lid and disturb the body of a man who left this world coughing up his lungs, unless there were serious suspicions, and nobody suspected me. That night we brought the dead man—a stranger who actually had taken his own life in Christiansted, and whose body no one had claimed—to your house. He was undoubtedly Puerto Rican, but not from Vieques. At least your father didn't recognize him. Neither did Estela, who knew almost everybody on the island. He spent the night in a room next to yours. Your mother prayed for him, lit candles for him, and thanked him for lighting the dangerous road I'd just successfully traveled. The next day we took him away with the help of two old people who pretended to be his parents, two of the dispossessed willing to pick up the body and bury it in a nameless grave. We gave them money and said he was a relative. They were tired and hungry, so they weren't surprised and didn't ask many questions. They only wanted to know if they should mark the burial place with a cross. Your mother was quick to answer yes.*

*On the first of January, 1950, we transported the weapons by sea to Fajardo. We welcomed in the year together and celebrated until dawn. You sang, Andrés. It seems to me I can see you and that gesture you used to make with your hat, imitating me. At about five or six in the morning, loaded down with fishing gear and a few bottles of brandy, we set out in a launch your father had rented. There were five of us, including the nationalists: the barber from San Juan, that man Roberto, and the fisherman at the helm. We acted drunk, sang, and vomited into the ocean.*

*On the afternoon of January 2, we returned to Vieques. Your mother embraced us as if she hadn't seen us for years. All of us, except Roberto. She didn't dare touch him, but she enveloped him in a look of such gratitude—that carnal, fiery gratitude filled with passwords—that I wanted to shake her. That night, when we were listening to the radio, she asked the barber to cut your hair. She brought a chair into the courtyard, and you sat down, a wretched look on your face because you didn't want anyone to touch your head. Your father and I lit cigarettes, and the* barber asked if we wanted to try his scissors too. We said no, almost in unison, and he said: "Well, it's your loss. The great heads of the revolution have passed through these hands."

He finished with you quickly; he gave you a crew cut. You passed your hand over your skull, rubbing it back and forth as if you were meditating. Then you asked who the "great heads" were that the barber had mentioned. I don't remember exactly what your father said, but I do know he didn't lie. It was the beginning of the worst year of your life. And of mine. Estela came over with a broom and swept up the hair he'd cut. We stood staring like idiots at the same spot on the ground: the locks of hair being pushed into the trash. It was like a magic spell; we kept staring at the scattered hair, and a great truth was revealed to us. Your mother, who continued to sweep, remained firm. But after a minute we men felt an emptiness, a sudden need to talk and to know we were alive. And that's what we did: we lit cigarettes, we opened bottles. We burned out at dawn.

# CHAPTER THREE

"I'LL be glad when you're dead, you rascal you." That was the song. I remembered some of it; something about stealing a wife and being gone.

My father, who grew up hearing English spoken in my grandmother Apolonia's guesthouse, helped me when I wanted to learn the song; he copied down the lyrics and then had me repeat them several times to correct my tone and pronunciation. I made an effort to imitate Armstrong's voice—he was Papá's favorite musician—and Papá encouraged me with his gestures and accompanied me on the guitar, which he had played since he was a boy.

If Christmas Eve was ours, and we almost never joined the guests, New Year's Eve was another matter. My mother and Braulia prepared the party, and early in the morning of the last day of December they'd send a vase of hibiscus and a pineapple decorated with a little flag to each room. On the flag they wrote the year that was about to begin, and next to it was a small card on which Mamá invited the guests to come celebrate in our house. The decorated pineapples for 1950 were the last ones they prepared.

The December guests were different from those in the summer, and the same people almost always were there. With us that year was a very elderly couple from Chicago who'd been coming to Vieques since their youth, first to my grandmother's guesthouse and then to my father's small hotel. There was also a retired ballplayer whose first name I don't recall but I do remember his surname, which was Green, we all called him Mr. Green; he was a former pitcher for the Orioles who'd grown up in Playa Grande, where his father was the doctor at the sugar mill, and who brought with him not only his wife and their son—a deaf boy with whom they communicated by signs—but also a black maid who was afraid of the waves. The most certain to show up each December was Gertrudis, the taciturn, muscular owner of coffee plantations on Isla Grande who always wore the same clothing: a black skirt and white blouse. Finally, there was a friend of my father's, like him the son of a Lebanese, a silent man almost always lost in thought, a jeweler by trade. As for J.T., his room was untouchable; he stayed in the same one year after year, and it even had a photograph of him in profile, a cigarette dangling from his lips, leaning against his plane, looking toward the La Esperanza reefs. You couldn't see them in the photograph, but he told me he'd posed looking toward that place because it brought back pleasant memories.

Two guests I'd never seen before in the hotel arrived on the last day of 1949, when Braulia was beating a meringue for the pie and Papá was chopping the ice. One of them, named Vidal, was a barber. After embracing him, my father waved me over. "Come meet a man."

The other was named Roberto, and when my mother heard from one of the maids that he was in the house, she dashed out of the kitchen. Her hands were covered in flour, and she wiped them off on her apron before greeting the newcomer, who was extremely tall, perhaps a little taller than J.T., who until then was the tallest man I'd ever seen. Braulia also greeted him, became a little flustered, and remarked that he looked thinner, and he murmured a phrase, but the only thing I could hear clearly was the word *prison*.

Then they remembered about me, and Papá caught my eye.

"Say hello to Roberto," he said. "You met him in Isabel Segunda."

I didn't remember him, but I thought it didn't matter because he held out his hand and kept looking at me. I thought he was smiling, but in fact it was an involuntary grin that was not particularly happy.

At that moment the Captain arrived, or perhaps he came a little later and I remember him in the midst of everyone, holding up a cluster of small lobsters and explaining their provenance: he'd brought them from St. Thomas though they'd been caught on Water Island. The old woman from Chicago wanted to see them up close, and the Captain held them right in front of her eyes, making her give little screams of craving and fear. Papá withdrew with the barber and Roberto, and Mamá returned to the kitchen with Braulia and J.T. Elodio Brito, the hotel cook, was at our house that day, helping to prepare the end-of-the-year menu. As soon as he saw the lobsters, he set a large pot of water on the stove, and while they were waiting for it to boil they began to talk about the nerve-wracking, strangely hot weather we'd had in December.

I stood in the door of the kitchen, waiting for the moment when they plunged the lobsters into the water, something I'd always enjoyed watching. But this time the animals let out a scream, an indescribable shriek of pain. J.T. was giving orders to the cook, and Braulia stood there mute, opening her eyes wide, as if she too had been submerged in burning hot liquid. The shriek didn't stop, and I walked into the kitchen: I stopped in front of my mother, who moved her head sadly. The Captain looked at me with impatience, as if it annoyed him to see me there, and he raised his voice to say that lobsters couldn't shriek, it was impossible for them to do that, and what we were hearing was only the sound of the shell contracting. I looked at my mother to see if she believed him, if the explanation satisfied her, and I discovered that she'd turned pale and was trying to

find something to hold on to, moving her hand through the air
without managing to rest it on my shoulder or anywhere else.
J.T. ran to her and grabbed her arms, because Mamá had begun
to sway, and finally I saw that her knees were buckling and he
was holding her up and blowing in her face, just at the height of
her lips; he barely brushed against them with his own lips,
which were so full and so greedy.

The shrieks of the lobsters were dying away, and my mother
seemed to come to in a world she didn't recognize. I tried to
catch Braulia's eye—I wanted to know if she'd seen it too—but
I realized she was hypnotized, looking alternately at the Captain
and at my mother, incapable of situating herself or identifying
the space where we happened to be, like ghosts floating in mist,
which was steam from the water where the lobsters were still
boiling, scalded red and completely silent. Mamá admitted later
that the heat had made her dizzy. The cook and Braulia went on
with their work. Nothing important or terrible had happened.
And yet I felt excluded and was filled with rage. A rage that grew
fainter as the hours passed, and disappeared completely when the
party began.

All the happiness in the world, which we would not feel
again for many years, descended on our house that night. Even
Gertrudis, a silent woman dressed in her eternal black skirt and
white blouse, was more communicative. In general she related
only to Braulia, who prepared a special menu for her every day,
different from the food she cooked for the other guests. But at
the party Gertrudis chatted for a while with my mother and accepted a glass of champagne from Mr. Green, the former pitcher
for the Orioles, a man with an enormous ass—Papá had told me
this part of the body was very developed in ballplayers. Gertrudis's
muscles, by contrast, resulted from her passion for the sea. She
spent almost the entire day at the beach, in the winter waves,
not quite as warm as the summer ones but full of foam and jellyfish. She was so strong a swimmer that on one occasion she

saved a fisherman whose boat capsized far out to sea; she brought him to shore and to safety, and then left to continue swimming. In those days she wore a cap over her hair, which was very short and coarse, tousled like a boy's. From one of the windows in the hotel, Braulia and I could see the orange dot of the bathing cap going up and down in the waves, sometimes disappearing completely. She would dry on the beach in the wind and sun because she never carried a towel, and she would come back completely dry, her hair bristling, the cap in her hand. Before she went into her room, she'd call to Braulia to bring her a cold drink. And the two would stay there talking, the door half-open, Braulia in the rocking chair—my father had put wicker rocking chairs in all the rooms—and Gertrudis sitting in front of her on the edge of the bed.

That year, my father's half-Lebanese friend seemed less distracted than at other times. He had been very young when he became a widower, and he had a young child, with whom he usually spent those days in December. But on this occasion, instead of bringing his son he brought a girl who looked very much like Santa, and I was sure she had the same breasts, not big and not small, just hot. He introduced her as his wife, though Braulia didn't believe it. I heard her when she told my mother that, as far as she was concerned, those two had gotten together just to welcome in the year; since it was 1950, everybody wanted to do something different. I felt a little embarrassed to sing and clown around in front of a girl like her, so different from all the other women who usually came to the hotel, but I'd already rehearsed the song and didn't want to disappoint my father, much less Mamá, who'd promised to sing a bolero as soon as I finished my imitation of Armstrong.

The party was well under way, and when I sang the song, J.T. looked at me like an old fox. I knew it was his signature song, the one he sang in the plane when he flew with us, and the one he sang with even more enthusiasm when he was transporting bodies because it tended to chase away the voices of the dead. "The voice is the last thing to go when somebody dies," the Captain once told us, and he explained it had nothing to do with ghosts or mocking spirits but had a scientific basis: energy was concentrated in sound itself, and the dead person's voice, a word, could remain floating around the body. That was why it seemed to the families of the deceased that they could still hear their dead. And in the silence of the night, as he flew from one island to another with a dead person onboard, he himself had heard that reminiscence of a voice clinging to the world.

When I finished my song, I saw that he was applauding, the look of an old fox still on his face. Then my mother sang a very sweet bolero in a small, husky voice, which was the only one she had, but at least she sang in tune. Then Papá began to play records, one after the other, and almost everyone danced except Gertrudis. The maids danced with the barber, who was there alone, and Roberto danced first with Braulia, who held herself rigid and made us laugh, and then just once with my mother; they danced to a song in English I can't remember now, but they did sublime turns and steps, like the ones they do in movies. The Captain danced very little, first with one of the maids, and then a bolero with the old woman from Chicago, not without first requesting her husband's permission. When my father put on a mambo, J.T. began to dance alone but changed his mind; he refused to continue even though people were asking him to. My father had drunk a little more than usual, which you could tell by the lock of hair hanging down over his forehead, and the Captain also asked his permission to dance with my mother. Papá nodded with a smile, and I thought of one of the lines from the song: "You mess with my wife, you dog." I repeated it when I saw him passing his arm around my mother's waist; the two of them, buoyant and full of hope, had forgotten about the world. Perhaps that was the moment I guessed their plans, and guessed at the tenderness of the Captain, who was in no way a tender man.

I drank too. Everyone was so enthralled by the arrival of 1950 that they forgot about the eleven-year-old boy who moved among the tables, and whenever a glass was in reach he'd drain the sweet wine or other liquor. Somebody stopped me to ask where I learned that comical song. It was Papá's half-Lebanese friend. I shrugged and continued on my way. The clock struck twelve just as I passed my father, who was standing and talking to the barber. In the midst of the uproar, Papá bent down to kiss me on the forehead. "Happy 1950, Andrés."

The barber patted me on the shoulder. "And long live the revolution, my boy!"

He said it quietly, and then he took a beret out of his pocket and handed it to me. "Now you're a cadet of the Republic. You put it on yourself."

The beret had a cross embroidered on the front. I was looking at it when I heard the Captain's voice behind me: "Keep our secret, Andrés."

I wondered if he was referring to the secret of the beret or talking about the other one.

"Don't tell anyone, understand?"

"You're not my father," I spat out, my lips almost closed so that nobody but him would hear me.

"What difference does that make?" he shot back. "I'm not your father, but in the war I might be your commander."

At that moment it made sense. Or at least it was the kind of remark that could disarm me.

"Don't talk to anybody about revolution, do you hear me?"

I lowered my head.

"Not anybody, okay?"

I looked up. The Captain was a giant. A living titan, endless and fierce.

"Okay," I replied.

# CHAPTER FOUR

IN January the soldiers began to arrive. They came from Panama, and we called them Panamanians, though most were from Puerto Rico, like us. Some hurried to find a girlfriend who'd be with them in their free time and, incidentally, do their laundry. Santa was perfect for that, and she became a soldier's girlfriend. Braulia told us at home and was very proud because the boyfriend belonged to the 65th Infantry, a regiment that had been famous since the Second World War.

On weekends we could barely make our way along the streets of Isabel Segunda, which were crowded with soldiers who couldn't get into the packed bars or cafés. Officers would come to Frank's Guesthouse in their jeeps with the excuse that they wanted a meal, but what they really wanted was to spend time with some girl. My father tried to keep them within bounds, and all over the hotel he hung signs indicating that there were no empty rooms. Even so, there was always one who insisted and showed his dollars so that he could stay. Braulia, dressed like a pious, churchgoing woman and not even wearing powder on her face, pretended to be the owner of the hotel and often managed to frighten away the intruders, who were young and didn't dare argue with an old, corpulent woman. On the other hand, those men weren't interested in squandering their money; it was a question not of insisting but of arranging a little hideaway where they could roll in the hay to their hearts' content.

That was how the first weeks of 1950 were for us. My father, as always, was mute; rather than mute, I'd say he was infuriated, even though the hotel was enjoying an unexpected bonanza. Traveling salesmen came to sell their wares, taking advantage of the fact that the island was full of soldiers—Braulia complained that they also were trying to sneak in contraband girls—and reporters would stay for a night or two, take notes on the maneuvers, and in the end, according to my father, publish very little about them in their papers.

One February morning, without warning, my mother didn't come to wake me. It was Papá, in his dark green pajamas, who did. I should have asked him why he was at home instead of buying fish in La Esperanza. But I think I inherited his tendency to few words and a minimum of questions. I got up and put on my school uniform, poured a glass of milk, then got into the truck. Papá was waiting for me with the motor running. At no time did I see my mother, who according to him had stayed in bed, which made me feel a mixture of sorrow and fear, of rage and fear, all combined; Papá's face expressed some indefinable sentiment.

If it had been Monday, we'd have stopped at Matilde's house to drop off or pick up the laundry. That would have helped me to think about something else. About how to be with Santa again, for example, and then I'd do it, I'd take off my shirt and then my trousers, strip naked the way that Marine had stripped. After our encounter in December, I'd seen her only a couple of times, and we hadn't been able to be alone on either occasion. On the Day of the Three Kings we happened to meet on the square in Isabel Segunda. She was wearing a street dress tied around the waist with a cord, and I knew right away she couldn't take it off as quickly as she took off her housedresses, pulling them over her head. She smiled at me, and I smiled back. As we did every January 6, we were taking some chickens as a gift to old Tana, the woman who'd worked the longest for my grandmother Apolonia, first in her guesthouse and then in the hotel, as both cook and housekeeper. Years later, when my grandmother got sick, Tana devoted herself to caring for her and didn't move from her side until they closed my grandmother's eyes. She'd spend the entire day listening to Apolonia's interminable deliriums about opening another guesthouse in Isabel Segunda. Though my grandmother's greatest delirium, at the end of her days, was to think that an old sweetheart of her youth, a revolutionary they called White Eagle, was coming to take her to his quarters on Isla Grande. Instead of White Eagle, the one who appeared, in her imagination, was my grandfather, the Lebanese costume-jewelry salesman.

"Not you." Apolonia would shoo him away. "What do you want here?"

She supposed the Lebanese had come to argue with her about the child. And by that time, since my grandmother could hardly recognize her son, Frank, in the large man with Arabic features, a prominent nose, and a black mustache, she took it into her head that I, who'd just turned seven, was her son. My grandmother would call me: "Come here for a minute, Frankie."

I'd answer that my name was Andrés and stand rigid, waiting for her to understand. Old Tana signaled to me to shut my mouth, and then, if my grandmother insisted that I approach, Tana came and took me by the arm, obliged me to stand in front of the bad-tempered old woman and listen to the gibberish she babbled when she thought she was speaking Arabic. When she spoke Arabic, it meant she was addressing my grandfather, the Lebanese trying to steal her boy from her. There were moments when she raised the volume of her gibberish so much that she was left exhausted, staring at her hands as they trembled with rage. My father assured me that the "Arabic" my grandmother spoke was only a sly invention, a phonetic imitation of the phrases and curses she'd heard the Lebanese say years ago. She struggled openly with my grandfather's ghost, whom she imagined pulling at one arm to carry me off to Lebanon, while she pulled at the other to make me stay. Naturally enough, I couldn't feel the ghost tugging at me. But I could feel Apolonia, her nails piercing my skin, her mouth muttering insults aimed at the man who was trying to take away the most precious thing she had in the world.

Generally Braulia would rescue me and quietly reprimand Tana for allowing my grandmother to mistreat me in that way. But sooner or later it would happen again. Unless Apolonia became melancholy, and instead of recalling the father of her child she'd travel much further in time, back to the period when she was seventeen or eighteen years old, and the only man in her life was the Eagle, whose band she wanted to join as cook or whatever else they needed, but she never did because he died before he could take her away. By this time my grandmother mixed up everything: children with grandchildren, love affairs with jewelry. She placed on the lips of White Eagle the verses that the Lebanese used to recite to her: Papá had said he was ugly but very romantic. "Passion in the heart," my grandmother would murmur, touching my chest with a fleshless finger, its nail yellow, "is like a tree with seven branches." She seemed to absorb the words from the air; she thought the Eagle was whispering them to her: "The first reaches the eyes"—and she would brush my eyelids—"the second reaches the tongue"—and she'd point at my lips, but I dodged her. Then she'd doze off, mumbling about the path of the other branches, and Tana would ask me to leave the room without making any noise. From the door I'd look at her again, feeling a mixture of amazement and repugnance. Amazement at the image of the tree, the mysterious trunk that still lived in her body, repugnance at her dead woman's fingers pointing at the invisible tree stirring awake inside me.

That morning in February, on the way to school, I wondered what kind of sadness my mother could be suffering that kept her from even getting up to say goodbye to me. And per-

haps because I'd remembered the Day of the Three Kings and
linked that memory to the one of old Tana and my grandmother Apolonia, the last of those verses came to mind: "The
sixth branch goes to the world; the seventh to the world beyond." I said this in my calmest voice, the one most incapable of
deceit. Papá didn't look at me right away; he kept his eyes on the
road, where suddenly there were a good number of Navy vehicles driving in the opposite direction.

"Who taught you that?" he said after a while. "It was your
mother, wasn't it?"

They were large trucks that raised clouds of dust. Traffic to
Isabel Segunda had been diverted, and we had to pull over to the
side of the road to make way for a kind of convoy. I asked my
father when we'd hear the bombardment. At that age, I looked
forward to explosions. The walls of the school would shake, and
the boys would shout and throw wads of paper at one another.
The girls, however, were afraid, or pretended to be very afraid.
In February 1948, when the Navy exploded the first bombs ever
heard in Martineau, Braulia disappeared into the kitchen. From
then on she lived through maneuvers with the constant dread
that one of the shells would miss its target and land on the hotel or the beach where we went swimming. To reassure her, my
father told her it was impossible. But the cook, who'd been in
the First World War, remarked that anything was possible when
there was gunpowder everywhere and so many soldiers frantic
to test their marksmanship. My mother was almost never afraid,
but for the first time she admitted that all she could think of
were the traps they were digging on the beach, the mines they
were burying, and all those instruments of war, unknown to us,
that they were setting around Martineau, all the way down to
the ocean.

"The bombardment," Papá murmured, not taking his eyes
from the convoy. "I suppose it'll start soon."

When the maneuvers ended, the waves would carry a blanket of dead fish to shore. When we left school, I'd go with my friends to collect them. We collected them and then threw them away, or made jokes with them among ourselves, since nobody could eat that fish. Along the coast we'd see the sharks, their fins destroyed but still moving their tails out of instinct, and sometimes we'd find a *tinglar*, the biggest of the tortoises, split in half with its guts hanging out, disdainfully moving its shattered head, close now to its longest sleep.

"There it is," said Papá, pointing at a truck carrying shapes covered with canvas. "I'll bet those are the bombs."

With the blanket of dead fish came the stink that saturated everything. You breathed the putrid air along the coast, then gradually it reached the streets and houses of Isabel Segunda. The stench enveloped Martineau as well, and the hotel filled with flies. To drive them away, Braulia placed large glass bottles filled with water in the windows. According to her, when the flies saw their reflections magnified in the bottles, they became frightened and went somewhere else. My mother fanned herself and complained that the foul smell took her breath away, and we'd continually hear Gerónimo roar and come into the house to tell us it wasn't worth touching a leaf, a branch, a single tree until the shelling was over because everything was covered with soot. My father turned away possible guests, murmuring that he'd rather have the hotel empty than risk hearing complaints about the explosions or the bad smell. He used the time to touch up the paint. Once a year we had to replace everything the saltpeter corroded. When I came home from school, Braulia would hand me a brush and a small can of paint and tell me to go over the wooden deck chairs because they were beginning to peel. These were hot afternoons filled with the winds of Lent, and sometimes, for hours on end, a deathly silence fell, a viscous stillness that would stick to our souls and that we endured as we thought about the next explosion, which might not be heard right away. Hours or days could go by, and then, when we least expected it, the ground would shake; first it would shake and then we'd hear the blast.

All morning at school I was thinking about Mamá without thinking anything concrete: I simply saw her and heard her voice saying unimportant words. At noon, when I went back to the house, she'd gotten out of bed, but only to lie down again on the wicker sofa in the living room. Her eyes were covered with a damp handkerchief, and I couldn't tell if she was really listening to the soap opera on the radio or was just allowing herself to be lulled by the murmur of the words. Braulia listened to the soap operas too—she always sat with my mother to listen—but since the end of January she'd stopped doing that. In fact, she didn't go out; she hardly talked at all—not even to herself, which she always used to do—and we didn't hear her arguing with the cook. I'd grown up hearing Braulia's chatter, and now I could hear only a silence you could cut with a knife, it was so thick and so filled with electricity. It was as if they'd put another woman in Braulia's place, a stupid stranger who wandered around the hotel, and sometimes around our house, but she did that less and less frequently. A mask had taken over her face, an unchangeable anguish not even my father could decipher.

"Estela," I heard him say one day, "do you happen to know what's wrong with Braulia?"

Mamá shook her head. I lowered my eyes, thinking she didn't know either, though I had a vague suspicion the change in Braulia had to do with something I'd seen on one of those afternoons when I was playing near the guests' rooms. And if my father had asked me, maybe I'd have told him that Braulia, who always brought a cold drink to Gertrudis as soon as Gertrudis came back from swimming, had thrown the glass to the floor. She didn't trip, and it didn't slip from her hands. Nothing like that. She threw it down on purpose, with a great deal of fury, at the foot of the rocking chair where Gertrudis was sitting, still in her bathing suit. After that, Braulia sat on the edge of the bed and began to cry. The other woman got up to look at the spattered sheets and the trail of broken glass. She was barefoot, but she held her bathing cap in one hand and walked calmly toward the balcony, as if she needed to go back to the beach. It was a hot afternoon, with patchy fog and very fine dust that darkened everything, but nobody knew where it came from. Braulia kept sitting there, her head lowered, sobbing with great emotion. Gertrudis came back from the balcony, picked up a towel, and stooped to push away the glass. Then she stood in front of Braulia, took her by the shoulders, as big and heavy as she was—so big-boned, as my father said—and forced her to her feet, the two of them facing each other, so close, so exhausted. They were almost the same height, and Gertrudis, who hadn't taken her hands from Braulia's shoulders, brought her body close, took a step toward her, their noses almost touching, their breasts too. That was when Braulia opened her lips and let a moan escape—from the place where I was watching them I thought it was a hiccup—then she turned her face away and ran out of the room. Gertrudis followed her with her eyes. When she did, she saw me spying on them but didn't say anything, she only slammed the door. But Braulia passed without noticing me, or without wanting it to seem that she'd noticed me. She ran down the stairs and took refuge in the kitchen.

"How were things in school?" Mamá said in her husky, almost invisible voice. She took the handkerchief away from her eyes and sat up to look at me. "I'm feeling better, Andrés," she added, as if she were answering a question I hadn't thought of asking. "Your father says you remembered the verses I recited to you when you were little."

"You didn't recite them," I protested, feeling somehow betrayed, "my grandmother Apolonia used to say them."

"And I did too," Mamá insisted, "because your father recited them to me when you were getting ready to be born. And your grandfather taught them to your father, and he learned them at home when he lived in Lebanon. A mystic wrote them, a saint."

Mamá got up and lowered the volume of the radio; she looked distracted and thin but at the same time very strong.

"We're going to San Juan the day after tomorrow. I'm going to the doctor, and your father will take you to see the Great Faster. Wouldn't you like to see him?"

The Great Faster was Urbano, the Hunger Artist, a man who'd gone inside a glass case and promised not to eat or drink a drop of water for twenty-five days. The radio was constantly announcing it, and wagers were being made in the newspapers on how long he could hold out.

"I want to stay here," I said, a desperate fury beginning to eat away at my throat, my heart, my bones. "They're going to start the bombardment."

"Stay here?" She blinked rapidly in disbelief. "There's nothing to see here but rotting fish and flies. How can you prefer that to going to San Juan with us?"

The case was on display in a theater, watched over day and night by witnesses who would confirm that the man had not eaten or drunk in all that time. At first, when I asked my father to take me to see him, he said that it was all a trick, that when nobody was looking they passed him soup through a straw. And that the real hunger artists were the dispossessed, who didn't charge to let people see them even though they had yellowed eyes and mangy skin and looked like sick cattle behind the fences where the Navy had put them. Even so, I insisted he take me to see the Great Faster; I wanted to ask him how anyone could live without drinking water.

"We could go to the movies too," Mamá said, knowing that was her best bait.

I stared at her, half-persuaded. I needed to ask her only one question.

"Is the Captain coming with us?"

"John?" she said in surprise, a false surprise. "You're going with your father and me, do you need anyone else?" She paused and sat down again on the wicker sofa. "Your Captain's in New York," she said in a quiet voice, and I don't know if there was any irony in what she said. "And in New York there's no water, they're having a huge drought. He won't be able to bathe until he gets back."

She smiled at her own witticism, which astonished me, and the news that the Captain was so far away left me somewhat dazed. Then she settled the pillow at one end of the sofa and lay down again, with the gesture of someone who wants to pick up the thread of the soap opera, which was concluding just at the moment when the name of a father would be revealed, the real father of I don't know who. The announcer came on to say that no one should miss tomorrow's installment. Mamá closed her eyes, placed the handkerchief over her eyelids, which were like onion skin. I thought the Great Faster slept that way too. Motionless, economizing, dreaming about his banquet, his secret food.

*IT happened in Rienzi's, a bar in the Village. No, not exactly a bar, and not a café either. It was something else; they called it a parlor, it was that kind of room, with sofas and mirrors and the music they always played there: religious songs, difficult Gregorian chants, the oldest ones known. I think the owner had been a priest, a monk, a Trappist deserter, someone who became tired of keeping silent. All I know is that Rienzi's was the fashionable place in those days. Students came there to drink their "tonics," tiny drinks that were pure syrup. We adults drank beer, sometimes whiskey. We spent the night telling jokes, laughing at any piece of foolishness, smoking, believing we were safe from horror, not thinking that another war was looming, the one in Korea. We still had that to go through.*

*I went to New York to visit my mother. After the divorce, she'd moved to Brooklyn with my stepfather and my sister, who at the time of the separation was only a few months old. I lived in Port Clyde with my father and a paternal aunt who took care of me when he had to travel to Washington. We lived like that until he and I moved to St. Croix. We were enough for each other; I was fifteen and had known how to fly since I was twelve. I'd see my mother once or twice a year, and when I became an adult, each time I went to New York I'd have a meal with her, though I never slept in her house but would go to the Village instead, to the apartment of one of my friends. In the afternoons we'd get together at Rienzi's. We avoided the subject of the war. I had volunteered as a pilot* but was sent back. As soon as we got to England, I developed a fever and my body became covered with pustules. The doctors said I had contracted some disease on the ship; they quarantined me for forty days, and when that period of isolation was over and I'd been transformed into a ghost, they sent me home. I had double vision, the result of the disease, and I wouldn't be able to fly for a long time. Some of my friends in Maine had died, and others preferred to move. That was the group in Rienzi's, the émigrés from Maine and the new friends they'd made in New York, all survivors of the war.

And so it was there—with that music in the background, the strange music of the living dead, because that, if you think about it, is what monks are—where everything suddenly seemed distant to me: my life on St. Croix, my flights around the islands, my visits to Vieques, even dawns at your father's little hotel. And not only distant but useless as well. All of it was old, confused, a landscape that was fading, dying in my mind and heart. Only your mother was still alive to me, only the memory of Estela had remained in my head, which now was empty, hollow, bereft of all feeling or any desire that wasn't desire for her. Outside it was growing dark, the boys were laughing around me (I say boys, but they were over thirty, like me), and one of them, a guy from the Bronx whose family was Greek, looked through the window, saw the streetlights go on, and asked for silence. He did that by tapping his glass with his spoon.

"But the night is beginning," he exclaimed in a very theatrical way, quieting the murmurs with a wave of his hand. "But the night is beginning now, and it would be good to obey it."

There was another instant of silence, and then an outburst of laughter and applause. That meant we were going out to look for women. But suddenly, for me, the line—it was a line from a poem, from a book by somebody or other—exploded in my mind. It made such a huge impact that I suffered an attack of vertigo, which I did my best to hide. I ordered another drink and lowered my head: it was not only a question of its growing dark and having to obey the darkness. What was suffocating me *was urgency, the sudden need to talk to your mother and ask her to run away with me that very week, or the following one, or in a month's time, a month at the most. We couldn't wait anymore. I couldn't, and I didn't want to. And the line, those simple words, had the effect of a hammer blow, it shook me inside. The typical ideas that came to mind, the ones you normally chase away when you're sober—that I could die anytime in the plane, for example, or that your mother could die—I didn't chase away then precisely because I'd had more to drink than usual, and because Estela's lack of sincerity, the way she'd been avoiding me since Christmas, had a devastating effect on me. I'd never experienced a feeling like that, not even when my mother abandoned me in Port Clyde, when I was seven or eight years old, not even then did it hurt so much to breathe, not even then did I feel I'd fallen so low, right down to the ground.*

*Later I took a walk through the Village for a breath of fresh air, and I thought the attack—I interpreted my anguish as a kind of epileptic attack—might be a sign that I was facing serious danger. I'd never paid any attention to presentiments; it was the first thing my father taught me before he let me sit my ass down in a plane: he warned me that you had to leave superstitions down on the ground. Most pilots behave that way; you'd have to get inside the skin of one of them: you learn to ignore dreams, and you learn to ignore certain hunches, because otherwise you'd never fly. I tried to ignore the gust of fear that had shaken me in Rienzi's, but I couldn't. Later, your father told me about it here, in Christiansted, while we were walking along these same streets, because if he was going to give me the details of his misfortune—which was mine as well—we couldn't remain seated, with a pitcher of beer in front of us, looking into each other's eyes. There are things that must be said while you're walking among people, just as you and I are doing now, not looking at any one spot, and stepping down hard as if you wanted to crush the torpor.*

*All of you had gone to San Juan that day, that afternoon when I was staggering around the Village. You and your father went to the movies,*

*I think. Your mother was seeing the doctor, that part is true: she went to the doctor because she was nervous, which in those days was almost the same as being pregnant. But it turned out to be a false alarm, or perhaps she miscarried in the hurry and rush of the trip. Something happened that kept her belly from growing, and kept your forbidden brother from showing his face, which would have been a face with the features of another man, maybe a revolutionary face. Your father was aware of everything and probably had a long conversation with Estela; she'd have told him some things, he'd have figured out the rest. That last part, made up of fragments, couldn't have been very pleasant, and he wanted to talk to me about his grief.*

*When I got back from New York, I went to Vieques, as I had so many other times, to bring in goods; I noticed the charged atmosphere, and I slept at the hotel, though it's an exaggeration to call it sleep. I spent the night nodding off, thinking about the conversation I'd have liked to have with your mother. The next day I went back to St. Croix, but first I had to stop in Tortola to pick up an envelope, a mysterious envelope that I had to deliver to a man whose boat was anchored in Christiansted. I left Vieques with terrible cargo: not only the certainty that Estela had closed the doors to me and had done it with disgust and with treachery but also the presence of your father, who insisted on flying with me but was in a rage, and more unmoving and silent than a dead man. He did look like a sleeper, a man with no return trip, a brute who doesn't even dream and whose only desire is that rest without images or pain.*

*He'd come out with occasional confused phrases. And the trip seemed eternal to me because we ran into a bad patch flying over St. Thomas; there were crosswinds, and for a moment I was worried and interrupted your father and told him we were going off course, and he asked if we had enough fuel to do that. They were tense minutes, but we were able to use them as a kind of truce. When we landed in Tortola and I turned off the engines, a great silence fell in the cabin. Your father said: "I'll be alone with Andrés. When that happens, I'll sell the hotel and go to work on St. Croix."*

*Silence on my part. It made me angry that he was simply worried about being left alone with you. It amazed me that he'd dare admit there was a world, a life, a child he'd have to continue caring for beyond the absence of your mother. What I'd experienced a month earlier in Rienzi's, that vertigo, I felt again there. I staggered as I got out of the plane, ran to some hedges growing along the runway, and vomited up my soul. Your father came toward me and handed me his handkerchief. I looked at him out of the corner of my eye and started to retch again, retching that was actually a deep sob, and he knew it. He grabbed my arms and forced me to look at him. What horrible thing could he have seen in these eyes, this mouth that still held traces of vomit, that made his expression change? It changed so quickly I couldn't dodge the first punch; it landed right on my mouth, and since I was so weak and dizzy, it knocked me to the ground. He picked me up, holding me by my lapels, and hit me again. "Son of a bitch!" he shouted and hit me a third time, on the jaw. A man who was watching everything, a guard at the small airstrip, approached with the intention of separating us. He said something like "You guys, what the hell . . ." Your father signaled to him to leave us alone. I was on the ground again, my lip was bleeding, and some drops of blood were running down my forehead; a few got in my eyes and blurred my vision. Frank squatted beside me, offered his handkerchief again, and since I didn't take it immediately, he stood up and threw it at my feet. He began to walk as if he were drunk, though he hadn't had a drop of liquor, I'm certain he hadn't. I wiped my face, stood up and spat, and then brushed the dust from my clothes. Curiously, I felt relieved; the vertigo had disappeared, and so had the nausea. And my feeling in general was peaceful, as if pain had settled in the place where it belonged. And doubts, all my doubts, had been resolved. My view was clear. Your father had cleared it for me with his punches. It's hard to confess sometimes that you need pain, a physical jolt, to see clearly what you need to see. You have no idea how much my ear hurt. And it kept hurting as we flew from Tortola to St. Croix, I with my mysterious envelope, your father with his face like a mask. An ordinary mask, nothing mysterious.*

*You, Andrés, came here to find out if the dreadful thing you saw, or imagined, was true. But your father didn't have to imagine anything about me; he didn't need to because he saw inside me. When he punched me in the face, it was because he saw what I'd been planning at Rienzi's. And he punched me because he had to get satisfaction from somebody. I'm an old man; if anybody threw a couple of punches like those at me now, he'd kill me. You're an old man too, and you don't have your mother; you don't even have the memory of a woman who chose to stay with you, who renounced her great love for your sake. You have doubts. Your memories are limited and confused because she died young and is too far away by now. That's why you probably don't see her as something that belongs to you.*

*We spent a few afternoons together. To be frank, I remember only five, and I'm sure I remember them all. We'd meet at the house of a friend of hers in Isabel Segunda, and from there we'd sneak away to Media Luna, to a hovel I rented for a couple of pesos. It doesn't matter now; nobody would remember it now. When my friends and I got together at Rienzi's, we were joined sometimes by a woman, the mother of a soldier who'd been killed in Normandy. She always looked a little dirty and was old before her time; she was only forty-seven or forty-eight but looked seventy. She'd drink with us, but never talked about her son, and often, when she was already drunk, she'd look at us with her glassy eyes and exclaim: "To hell with it all, in fifty years nobody will remember any of this."*

*Poor thing, she didn't count on my recalling her here, so far from the Village, and facing a man full of anger. Nothing surprises you anymore because you're blinded, obsessed by that afternoon's mistake. It's the only thing that interests you, perhaps the only thing that keeps you alive. Or maybe it's just the reverse, and all this time you've been dead, or like a dead man. I know you haven't been able to enjoy your life. Last night I couldn't catch my breath, and for a moment I thought I had no time left to kill the ghost, to pull the rusty nail out of your old bald head that's not much more lucid than mine.*

*There, along Church Street, a street that people in the 1940s still called Kirke Gade, there was a place where we'd take you for ice cream. You'd come with your father and me, or with your mother and me, and we'd buy you the special ice cream they made with milk from a red cow that had no horns and was raised only on St. Croix, on the farm of a man called Bromley. I knew him because he was a friend of my father's, and I went to see his cattle very often. They said the cow produced milk that was half sugar and that's why the ice cream was so delicious, but I never tasted it. When I came to live in Christiansted, when I was still a boy, they didn't make it. And later, when we came with you, I didn't feel like eating ice cream anymore. I felt old, maybe that's what ruined me: after thirty I turned into a predictable type, a vain man who passed himself off as an adventurer but all he wanted really was to sit on his ass. It hurts me as much as it does you, it still hurts me somewhere, but Estela loved me only in the sense that she also loved your father. And as you must understand, for me that was too little. The bliss, the unbearable bliss was taken away by that poor wretch, so different from us, truly an uncapturable man (he was for Estela) who died of eighty-four bullets, eighty-four shots to his chest and back. They say the body dissolved like gelatin when they tried to pick it up from the ground.*

*And all of it, that cruelty, was with your mother when she closed her eyes. I'm sorry to tell you that your kiss wasn't with her—you kissed her on the hand, I don't know if you remember that. And Frank's tears weren't with her—in the end he began to snivel beside her bed. She didn't even want my rage and my desire to live, my tremendous avidity. I put it all at her disposal, in her eyes and her hands, because I believed if she accepted me there, accepted that whisper of life in the midst of all her death, she'd pull me along with her, take me wherever she wanted, with God or the devil. I left the room where she died, took off in the plane, and tried to crash it in La Esperanza. But I couldn't. She stopped me, she didn't let me kill myself. Not even then did she want me with her. She went off with the other one; finally she achieved that. You and I are two creatures as abandoned as your father.*

*Hours later I returned to the hotel. Braulia had gone out with Frank to buy the coffin. But before she left she washed Estela's body, and the whole room smelled of patchouli, a mixture of patchouli and camphor. I haven't forgotten the smell. Your mother was a perfect sleeper, because the most perfect are the ones that look dead. And she did, but in what an unusual way. Her hair was intact, suspended over the pillow, swelling with animal fury, as if it were a mane. It was hair that had retained its voice. In the darkness, it seemed to me it was speaking.*

# CHAPTER FIVE

THE Greatest Faster in the World opened his eyes and looked into mine. It happened just as I leaned over the case, so that the first thing he saw was my face, my ecstatic glance waiting for a gesture, the slightest movement of his doll's body. He had a bony, hairless face, and ears that were too small and twisted, their color darker than the rest of his skin. He was dressed only in a pair of white trousers, held up at the waist by a kind of rope. The chest of Urbano, the Hunger Artist, was sunken, as if someone had delivered a blow, a punch that had displaced heart and bones and left for all time a hollow, an unsettling concavity covered by very delicate skin.

Behind me people were waiting in line for a turn to have a look at him, and Papá whispered to me to move on, but I didn't budge. I stiffened my body instead and clutched at the railing that encircled the case. Then Urbano opened his colorless mouth; you could see he was trying to speak but not a sound came out. Papá tugged at my arm and accompanied his tugging with words that resounded through the theater: "Move, Andrés!" This was the only way he could drag me to the spot where people were waiting who'd already seen the Faster's face but still were hoping for something more—they wanted to hear him speak. A man wearing glasses and dressed in a blue suit approached the case, accompanied by a guard. Papá said the man was a famous journalist, and the guard's job was to move people away so he could interview Urbano. We were all sweating because the fans couldn't move enough air, or the only air they moved was hot. But the journalist, encased in his double-breasted suit, was sweating more than anybody, and I saw that his head was streaming with perspiration, as if someone had taken revenge by throwing a bucket of water at him. Miraculously, Urbano didn't sweat, and he didn't look tired either, just sad and somehow dusty. The journalist turned toward the public and asked us to be quiet because the Faster wanted to say a few words. The line stopped moving, and all of us paid close attention, but Urbano's voice couldn't be heard. People began to complain, some crowded around the railing, ignoring the guard's warnings, and the journalist, fearing they would overturn the case, intervened again to ask for calm, explaining that the Hunger Artist spoke very quietly in order not to waste his strength but had said he felt fine and was grateful for our presence there. At that moment someone began to applaud, and we all joined in except my father, who became very somber and stood with his arms folded. Two more guards began to empty the hall so that a new batch of spectators could come in. Papá complained that we had gotten very little for the fifty cents we had paid: thirty for his adult ticket and twenty for mine, since I was still a child.

We left the theater and began to walk through Santurce, a part of the city where we'd never walked before; we always walked in the old district on the few occasions we came to San Juan, a trip that in those days was as complicated as traveling to another country.

"Do you remember Vidal?" Papá asked suddenly, "the barber who came to the hotel?"

I said I did. The way he'd cut my hair, almost shaved it with no compassion at all, still caused me grief.

"Well, we're going to his shop," he said. "I want him to give me a trim."

We were walking quickly, and from time to time my father took off his hat to wipe the perspiration from his forehead and the back of his neck. When he took it off, I looked at his thick, black hair and thought about what the barber would do with the rebellious lock that fell to one side. I wanted to ask if I'd have to have my hair cut too, but I was afraid he'd say yes and I changed the subject, asking instead if he really thought Urbano could spend twenty-five days without eating or drinking. Papá answered that nobody could survive that long without food, much less water. "He wants to earn money to buy himself a good steak," he said. "That's all the poor devil wants."

I imagined the Faster sitting at the table after his long fast, devouring a filet that was almost raw, like the ones served to the guests at the hotel when they wanted their meat rare, red on the inside, full of blood.

"It's probably a trick," Papá suggested, "and they pass him a little sugar water in secret. But I'll bet the only thing he wants is to eat a good piece of meat. Listen, Andrés: we all want something that we pretend we don't want."

I must have been obsessed back then, because I asked myself if he said that because of my mother, because of how lethargic she'd become, when all she really longed for was to fly away, to escape the hole of Martineau and leave us another filthy hole: the hotel and its guilt—I'd always feel guilty. Or did he say it because of J.T., with his air of not needing anything at all from other people, of not loving anybody? Who knows if he was referring only to how, just three or four days earlier, I refused to go with him to Matilde's house to drop off the bundles of dirty laundry? The desire to see and touch Santa had vanished, and in its place I felt a kind of rage that paralyzed me. I wanted to go back to the way it was before, waiting for her in the little shed with the bleach and watching her undress. Forget that I could take off my shirt, fall on her body again, die without moving. But I couldn't forget that. There was no going back.

"There's the barbershop," Papá said at last, and he pointed at the sign that said SALÓN BORICUA.

When I went in I smelled the scent of cologne. The barber smiled at my father but remained concentrated on his work: he was cutting the hair of a little boy, a belligerent black kid who kept kicking while his mother held him. Papá sat down and picked up the paper; I went out to the street and watched the people, the peddlers, the children running around the sidewalk, the life of the Barrio Obrero, a life so unlike my life of beaches and solitary games, so different from the world of the ocean, which is another unending world. After a while, the black kid passed me and I looked at his head, almost bald and covered with nicks. Papá called to me from inside. "Andrés, come say hello to Vidal."

The barber held out his hand. "Have you worn the beret yet?"

He was referring to the beret of a cadet of the Republic that he had given to me at the New Year's Eve party. I nodded yes, though it wasn't true; my mother had put it away and forbidden me to wear it to school. I thought I'd be bored in the barbershop, so I asked my father if I could wait for him outside.

"Don't go far," he said. "Somebody's coming and I want you to meet him."

But in fact I did go far. I walked a few blocks and was thinking about the Hunger Artist, wondering how he urinated or moved his bowels, and if someone had the job of watching him so he couldn't drink even a drop of his own urine, which was what shipwrecked people did. I had that image in my mind, of the Faster urinating in front of reporters, and without being able to help it wasting all the liquid left in his veins, when I felt somebody touch me on the shoulder. I turned around. It was a very fat man dressed in a suit and wearing a striped tie covered with stains.

"You're Vidal's son?"

I shook my head. The man's face was oozing grease, and his nose was like a botched fritter, rough and shapeless.

"What do you mean no?" he insisted sarcastically. "I saw you in the barbershop. You just walked out of there."

I denied it again. He reeked of sweat.

"Then did you go for a haircut, or did you go with your father?"

"For a haircut," I said, a lie that came from my instincts.

"And who's your father, if you don't mind my asking."

I thought about starting to run, but he seemed completely prepared to block my way. I told another lie, another story born of instinct.

"My father's name is John Timothy Bunker," I said, "and he's a combat pilot."

His smile froze. He stared at me, looking for a chink, a tiny crack in my face, which until then, I suppose, had conveyed self-assurance.

"So it's Bunker, hmm?" he muttered. "And your name is . . ."

I tightened my lips. The man had a scant mustache, and in the corners of his mouth there was a kind of white gelatin, saliva that was old and sticky.

"What's your name?"

"Andrés!" I shouted and ran in the opposite direction from the barbershop, and maybe this time I did go too far. After a while I looked back and the man had disappeared. I turned and tried to get back to the Salón Boricua as fast as I could, running past the people, avoiding the fruit stands and horse-drawn wagons—there were still wagons in those days. Long before I arrived, I could make out the white hat worn by my father, who was waiting for me in the doorway of the barbershop. He saw me approach but didn't walk toward me or make any gestures; he could tell from my face that something had happened.

"A man," I blurted out, still breathless from running, "he asked if I was the barber's son, he wouldn't let me go."

My father looked up and down the street and simply said: "Go in."

As soon as we were inside, Vidal hurried to close the barbershop's metal shutters. "We finish at six," he said in a low voice. "It's a quarter to."

There were no other customers, and he offered me a cold drink. Papá asked, very casually, what exactly the man had said to me. I told him part of the conversation, omitting the lie born of instinct: I didn't dare tell him I'd said my father was J.T., a combat pilot.

"Did you say we weren't from San Juan?"

I looked at Papá and then at the barber, who was also waiting for my reply. I looked back and forth at the two of them, trying to devise a neutral answer that would sound childish.

"Drink your soda," I heard my father say. "We'll talk later."

We went to the back room, the barber pulled aside a curtain, and the first thing that came out was smoke. Two men were smoking, and the figure of a third, who wasn't smoking, came toward us.

"I'll introduce you to Don Pedro," said my father. "Don Pedro, this is my son, Andrés."

Pedro Albizu Campos was the head of the nationalists. He had a sallow, compact face that gave the impression everything had been carried to the limit: his forehead, his cheekbones, his mustache, his cleft chin. He had a lion's mane of hair, curly and disheveled, and I supposed that was why he was in the barbershop. His jacket was open, and he'd already loosened his tie. I had a feeling that if I looked at his feet, I'd see a pair of enormous shoes, like a clown's. I looked at them on the sly and discovered just the opposite: his feet were rather small, encased in worn shoes, diminutive shoes from another time, with faded laces.

"When the moon's full, you plant only squash or celery," Don Pedro said, returning to who knows what conversation. "For everything else, you have to wait for the waning moon."

He'd stopped in front of me, and I suspected he was staring at me. I didn't know anything about moons or planting. I couldn't even imagine why he was talking to me about those things.

"Tonight it begins to wane. Pleased to meet you, Andrés."

It was a small, hard hand, like an agile crab, that shook mine, and when I glanced up to look into his eyes, I swear I saw the eyes of the Great Faster. The smoke enveloped both of us, and for a moment I had the feeling I was looking into another world, another case, a territory of immobility just like the one that belonged to the Hunger Artist. He gave me a big smile, and now I think there was a certain femininity in those full lips, their tone softer than the brown of his face.

"We'll go now," said my father, but before he left he took the barber aside and spoke to him in a low voice.

We left by the back door, and Papá said we'd take a taxi. It was getting dark, and my mother was waiting for us in her sister's house; my aunt Manuela was a calm, older woman not as pretty as Mamá and, I imagined, less apt to lead a double life: the one on the surface and the other one, the one trembling in a secret place that few people could imagine. I thought we still had the next day to go to the movies, or to go back to the theater. I was certain my father wouldn't want to see the Great Faster a second time, but I might be able to persuade my mother or one of my cousins to go with me.

"The man who asked you questions," Papá whispered so the cabdriver wouldn't hear him, "I want you to know he was a policeman."

I shook my head. Papá kept talking in whispers.

"Not all of them wear a uniform, Andrés, but they're policemen. Did you tell him your name?"

"I told him my name was Andrés." I spoke with my mouth to his ear. "And that J.T. was my father."

A great weight had been lifted from me, and it must have been visible in the expression on my face and in how I relaxed my arms. Papá was very quiet, and then he turned toward the window and looked out at the streets until we arrived. Before we went into my aunt's house, he glanced at the cab, which was quickly driving away down the narrow streets.

"Good. Did you say Bunker?"

"I said Bunker. I said my father was a pilot."

Mamá was in bed, and my aunt told me to wash my hands and go in to see her. Papá had taken off his hat, and his hair was intact, he wasn't even missing the rebellious lock that still fell onto his face. The two of them moved away; my aunt took him by the arm but didn't say a word. I realized she was waiting for me to leave so she could talk to him.

I reached the room where my mother was resting with her eyes closed; I went over to her and saw that she was wearing a sleeveless nightgown. First I looked at her arms, thinner than I expected, and at the whimsical, almost vegetal way they were attached to her body. Then I looked higher and saw that one of her nipples was visible through the half-open nightgown. She heard me breathing and opened her eyes; she covered herself quickly and asked what I had thought of the Faster.

"He was lying down," I replied. "He spoke very softly and I couldn't hear him."

Mamá smiled and took my hand. I was afraid of what she might say.

"He must be very hungry," she said with a sigh. "Tomorrow they'll hear him a little less. And the next day even less, and on and on until he's mute."

She brought my fingers to her mouth as if she too needed nourishment. She kept them there, and the little current of her breathing seemed like something liquid, something profound and slow that was leaving her.

"THIS city is like a sad Sunday," declared the Captain, and he looked around him as if he didn't recognize or understand anything. "Do you remember how all of this was when we used to come here with your father?"

He grimaced and closed his eyes. The light bothered him; redheads have always been bothered by excessive light. But I also had the impression he was attempting to evoke an image. Or perhaps he was sure, secretly, that when he opened them the landscape of those years would be superimposed on this one: this sleepy Christiansted with its deserted streets and half-empty stores, and some of its houses, the magnificent houses from that time, in ruins.

"It seems it never recovered from the hurricane," he said with a sigh, his head lowered. "What was the name of that awful hurricane?"

I remained silent because suddenly I was overcome by the absurdity of the situation: John Timothy Bunker, a dying reprobate, walking beside me along King Street as if we were friends, or father and son, the father very old and frail, with his son, less old and less frail but equally defeated as he faced the void.

"Maneuvers began the end of February," he said suddenly. "I remember I'd just come back from New York then, and I promised to take you to see the paratroopers, a thousand paratroopers who'd jump at the same time. I kept the promise. You were full of excitement."

Excitement and fear, because I knew something inside our house was collapsing and nobody could stop it. When we returned to Vieques after our trip to San Juan, Mamá made an effort to resume her ordinary life. She sat down to sew more frequently; she went with me sometimes to the beach and was constantly going into the hotel kitchen to help with the meals or suggest ideas, recipes she'd read in the papers and cut out and paste into a notebook. My mother always liked the kitchen, but during this time she took refuge there as if she were searching for something else, a sign in the open flesh of the animals, that absurdly quiet and often bloody flesh.

Papá also threw himself into his routine: going for fish at dawn, supervising the work of the maids with Braulia, keeping the guests' registration book, taking care of the many things that needed to be repaired in a place like that, where the saltpeter licked away at the walls and the locks and, if we weren't careful, eventually turned anything left outdoors into dust.

"The Third Division was there," the Captain recalled, "and the Navy, with everything they had. For the first time you could see jet planes. Plus tanks and ships and the eighty thousand soldiers who landed. No less than eighty thousand, Andrés, all of them in a frenzy to shoot their weapons."

We stopped at a bar. The Captain was short of breath and had turned pale. I wondered what I would do if he collapsed in the middle of the street. It happens to people with terminal cancer; sometimes their hearts stop, an act of mercy taken by their own organism. For a moment I imagined asking bystanders, a couple of cabdrivers leaning against the wall of an old bodega, killing time, for help. I'd have to take him to the hotel and find his telephone numbers in Maine. I realized I didn't know who this old man lived with, if he was married or had children, grandchildren. If he did have a wife, she was an old woman who hadn't been able to stop him from making the trip and was now consumed by anxiety while she waited for him in their house in Port Clyde.

"They simulated a huge battle between the regiments from Norfolk that supposedly were going to defend the island and the men of the 65th Infantry, who pretended to be enemies who were occupying it. Your father's hotel was caught on the frontier of that hell. He couldn't accept any guests for three weeks."

But I remembered that he did: in the midst of those maneuvers, in spite of the bombs exploding day and night, and the planes that seemed to disintegrate over our heads, one person insisted on coming to Frank's Guesthouse, begging my father to take her in as a guest and assuring him that the noise and discomfort didn't matter. It was Gertrudis, the woman in whose room I'd seen Braulia behave so strangely and then become so mournful, transformed into everything she hadn't been before. Gertrudis, who'd left at the beginning of January, reappeared, for the first time, when it wasn't Christmas. And for the first time she brought a gift for our house from her farm, a detail that softened her: pheasant chicks that Braulia helped me care for.

"I was only interested in seeing the *Missouri*," the Captain ruminated, like a child dusting off an old whim. "I was only interested in that battleship, which was famous back then. I didn't care about the paratroopers, but you were crazy to see them, and your mother begged me to find a way to take you. She knew they were distributing passes for the platform where you could watch them come down. Your mother imagined that, since I was an aviator and a gringo, I could get them. All she wanted was to please you. Before she left you, she didn't think about anything but making your life happy."

I looked down. At moments like these I felt capable of squeezing the Captain's neck, seeing him plead with his eyes, his tremulous, encrusted little eyes, and still keep squeezing, harder and harder, with infinite hatred, until I made him spit out my mother's name.

"It was like D-Day, the day of the paratroopers. It was very difficult to get passes, but I still had some friends in the Army, and a few acquaintances in the Air Force. I'd never asked them for a favor before, that was the only one. Braulia woke me at dawn—you were already awake—and the two of us left in Eugene the Jeep, that's what we called my Willys. On the way you asked me something about the C-82s, the planes we'd seen a little earlier flying over the airport. And suddenly you sprang it on me without any preamble; you said it as we were getting out of the Jeep, as if you were hoping to see me fall, as if you'd enjoy that: 'Estela doesn't love you anymore.' It was so unexpected that all I could answer was: 'I know. Neither do you, or your father, or that damn Braulia. Nobody can stand me in Martineau.' I started walking but didn't hear your footsteps behind me, so I turned to see where you'd gotten to. Then I caught your expression—full of loathing, adult, bristling with defiance: 'The fact is that Estela hates you much more than Braulia does.' I put my hands on my hips and walked toward you. I made sure I could look down at you. 'Fuck you,' I said, and I tousled your hair and almost had to push you to make you walk. When we arrived, all the seats were taken and we sat on the grass. You didn't say another word, you waited in silence, like me and like the rest of the people, sipping lemonade from a thermos your mother had insisted we take."

Lemonade, of course. The Captain's memory was intact. At least the part of his memory that went back to the year where we became frozen: we were still there, cold and defeated. As for me, I hadn't forgotten that image either: the planes approaching from the north, and the thousand men who jumped into the void. The Captain and I kept behind a barricade, but he had binoculars, and at one point he gave a start and said he thought one of the paratroopers had been carried by the wind and probably was heading out to sea. I asked if they would rescue him, and he said it was very difficult because the weight of his gear would pull him right down to the bottom. Then he looked at me, put his hand on my shoulder, as if the hypothetical death of the paratrooper struck both of us with the same asphyxiating stupor and in the same heartrending place. It was a microscopic instant of complicity, but that instant was enough: I sensed a hidden strength in him, a capacity for understanding that justified everything my mother might feel. That justified, in short, her preferring him to my father or me.

"Nobody imagined another war was coming," the Captain murmured, looking straight ahead at the bottles that had collected along the barricade and reconstructing in them a hidden landscape in the dust. "Who could have told us that Korea was around the corner? It took us by surprise. My friends from Maine, who were gradually leaving New York, and the friends they'd made there. I suppose Rienzi's emptied out. I couldn't go back."

I ordered a Haitian rum I'd never had before; the bottle had a red label with a gray skull. I felt I needed something strong and thought this liquor from beyond the grave might be it.

"You're drinking that now?" the Captain asked ironically.

"You don't know what I drink," I said, returning the irony.

"Excuse me," he said with a smile. "Do you know that for a moment I confused you with your father? I spoke to you as if you were Frank. That happens with cancer, there's a moment when we feel we're finished and begin talking to the dead, to those we loved most."

I shook my head in disbelief. I drank down my rum in one swallow and ordered another. The Captain ordered the same thing.

"After watching the paratroopers, we ate hot dogs with the rest of the visitors. We spent a long time there, and I was happy about that, because the next day everything good turned to sadness for you." He paused. I was afraid he'd begin to say what he said: "If it helps you at all, I always knew who the two men were who mangled that girl."

I gazed at him without answering and looked into his eyes, two rheumy slits in the midst of all those wrinkles. What kind of rat spends time with a horror like that only to delay his confession of another horror?

"She disappeared the same day we went to see the paratroopers. And they found her the next day, near the lighthouse at Punta Mulas. Do you remember her name?"

Santa, I thought, but I didn't feel like telling him. I didn't want him to say that name too. It would have been too hard, or too sordid.

"Somebody pointed out the two guys who did it, it was in a bar in the Destino district. Somebody said, 'Do you see those two? . . . It was them.' They were leaning on the bar, pretty drunk, drinking everything put in front of them. They still had scratches on their faces."

I kept staring at the Captain. I wanted to ask him to change the subject, to talk to me again about the battleships, the paratroopers, the decisive battle fought that day; even at night no one could sleep in Martineau because of the smoke. But I didn't dare; I really wanted to hear the rest, recover Santa in one piece: the living part that I knew but also her death. I needed to know the circumstances of her murder, the circumstances my father never wanted to discuss with me.

"They ripped off her nipples with their teeth. They scalped her, they did that while they were dragging her along on the ground. She was still alive."

I'd like to remember her hair. It was dark brown, but I can't recall how long it was or how thick it was to the touch. The day before her disappearance, I went with my father to pick up the clean laundry for the hotel, and it was my father who encouraged me to walk around the courtyard while he drank some coffee. Now I understand that he knew everything, knew I used our visits to go into the shed with the washerwoman's daughter; he applauded it to himself, these are things fathers applaud in their sons. But that day, Santa and I only kissed. She looked happy and was wearing intense orange lipstick. I tried to touch her, to put my hand under her skirt, as I'd done on other occasions, but she wouldn't let me. There are certainties one cannot assume at the age I was then; instead a small rage arises or a small, irrefutable intuition. I sensed she was saving herself for someone else, someone not like the Marines and certainly not like me: after all, I was only a boy.

After we kissed, and my face—above all my cheeks and chin—was smeared with her lipstick, Santa said I couldn't go out like that but had to wait and clean up a little. With her saliva she dampened a corner of the same little towel she always used to dry herself off after being with the Marines, and while she was cleaning me she said that the night before she'd had a dream about the rinse water for the laundry, which normally took its color from the bluing, but in her dream the water was dark and came up to her neck. Then I took from my shirt the present that I had brought for her from San Juan; it was an autographed photograph of Urbano, the Hunger Artist, and she kept looking at the photo, asking herself how anybody could live for so many days without eating or drinking.

"It wasn't the Marines," the Captain revealed, turning slowly toward me, and then I detected the odor from his throat, the odor of stagnant water. "It was a fat second lieutenant and another guy, a corporal who was almost always with him. Nobody dared lay a finger on them. The police blamed one of the dispossessed, a man who was half-crazy and lived in the vicinity of Punta Mulas. Then the crazy man hung himself, and that was the end of the problem. That was the end of the girl too. You really can't remember her name?"

"Santa," I whispered, more to myself than to the Captain.

"Ah, Santa," he exclaimed. "Two days later I talked to Estela."

I raised my head; it was the instinctive reaction of a deer that catches the scent of a nearby hunter. My tongue felt pasty, as if Santa had given me a goodbye kiss right there and the taste of her lipstick—dried out and bitter, rotting on her rotting mouth—had gone down my throat.

"Now," I rebuked the Captain, "let's get to what brought us here. Not what you said to my mother but what you did to her afterward."

I listened to him order his second glass of rum. He closed his eyes in order to see better. March 1950. There's the sound of planes passing over the hotel, the deafening noise of bombs falling to the north, but very far to the north, in the place where Hodgkins Reef used to be, which now is only an awful crater. There's a scorched smell in all the rooms. Mamá's in the kitchen, probably by herself. It's four or five in the afternoon, and the cook has taken a few days off; Papá gave him the days since the hotel is empty. Or almost empty. We have Gertrudis in one of the rooms overlooking the beach, but Braulia cooks for her. And my mother cooks for us, for my father and me. The maids work only half a day. They clean the one room that's occupied, Gertrudis's room, and then they come to our house to clean too; they've always done that, but they do it with more reason these days, now that Mamá's so lethargic. I'm in the courtyard in my Zorro costume—the cape, the mask, the black shirt—but I'm also wearing the beret the barber gave me, the beret of the cadets of the Republic that my mother has allowed me to wear just for today, just for this afternoon, since the employees aren't around and Gertrudis and Braulia won't tell anybody they saw me with it. Besides, neither of them will come to our house until seven or eight at night, after we've eaten. Only then do they venture out of their retreat for a little air, even if it's the tormented air of the maneuvers filled with strange particles, the remains of the burning and the remains of the slaughter.

The Captain walks past me and makes a move to touch me

but changes his mind (because of the beret he can't muss my hair). He asks for my father, and I tell him he went to Isabel Segunda. He looks at me, the kind of look that really rests not on me but on what I am, a momentary hindrance, a stupid witness. Then he goes straight to the kitchen; he's huge, and determined. I get to my feet, take off the beret, and stand looking at him. I feel a tightening in my chest, as if I'm not breathing in enough air through my mouth, or not enough is getting down to my lungs. I wish Papá were there. Or that he'd come back unexpectedly. I wish Braulia, she at least, would suddenly appear looking for a cup of milk, a pinch of oregano, anything she couldn't find in the hotel kitchen and usually gets from the kitchen in our house.

"I reproached her for having left me," the Captain finally vomited up. "And she expressed her feelings to me and spoke with a cruelty I've been able to understand only now, when I'm dying too and can be pretty cruel to other people. Estela saw the future even then. She saw her death coming."

I thought that if I killed the Captain then, or slapped him and threw him to the ground, in his condition it would be like killing him and I wouldn't learn the second half of his story. I squeezed the glass; for an instant I almost heard it cracking, but the glass resisted.

"That day I found her in the kitchen. Recently Estela had taken refuge quite often in the kitchen. The one in the house, of course, but the one in the hotel too, displacing the cook and Braulia, who in her old age had become a pervert and taken a girlfriend, a dyke who came to the hotel every year and who, since she was a landowner, took her away in the end, dragged her off to Isla Grande and locked her away on one of her plantations."

The Captain licked his lips, or that was his intention. Instead, he passed his dry, metallic tongue over the open crack where there once had been lips, a lying, miserable mouth.

"As soon as she saw me that day, your mother asked me not

to say what she knew I wanted to talk to her about. She explained that her husband and son were in the house, and it was time for me to accept that what had been between us had vanished; friendship quieted everything, and she intended for us to be friends. I replied that, in case she didn't know it, her husband had gone to Isabel Segunda, and it was true her son was outside, but he was very involved with his Zorro outfit and his cadet's beret. There was irony, a malicious charge in what I said. There was jealousy, which was the main thing. And the conviction that your mother was using me. What was a man like me, born in Maine, the son of a war hero, doing mixed up in illegal weapons with a gang of nationalists who had nothing to do with me and who, if they caused any feeling at all in me, it was pity for a miserable revolution that in a blink of the eye would turn into suicide. Listen to me: if your father was not completely involved, it was because Estela held him back. You were only eleven and she knew that you would be without her, and she didn't want you to be without your father too, so her decision to leave changed everybody's plans. She asked your father to lay low, or protect himself better, and he understood and promised he'd survive to take care of you."

I felt dizzy. Too much rum, too much heat, too many shadows in the Captain's words.

"What did you finally talk about with my mother?"

He was sweating, livid, strangely cheerful. He'd had too much to drink as well.

"What did you finally talk about with my mother?" he repeated in an anxious tone that imitated mine. "You sound like a faggot, Andrés. What do you think I talked to her about? I asked her to leave everything. And the everything she had was your father and you, or that's what she wanted to prove. I proposed she come with me to St. Croix, to my little beach house on Chenay Bay. And do you know what she did? She burst into laughter and said she wanted to be buried in the cemetery in

Isabel Segunda where her mother was buried. It made her sick to think that if she died far away, I'd have to put her body in a shroud and carry it in my plane back to Vieques. These were desperate lies. She said she was afraid of what would happen to her corpse, and how your father would react when she came back, a dead adulteress. She said she was particularly afraid of what would happen to you, of what you'd have to see."

"You know what I saw." I pushed my body against his. "Something more horrible, much more sickening than anything she could imagine."

The Captain rose to his feet, staggered, and I held him up by one arm, but I did it with animosity, with so much violence he couldn't repress a grimace of pain.

"I'm urinating," he said, but he didn't move, he couldn't take a step. His khaki trousers were wet, and a little puddle of urine formed at his feet, dripping onto his tennis shoes.

"I got sick," I whispered, "and it still turns my stomach."

"My life ended that day, Andrés. I got sick too. A sickness that's lasted fifty years. Tell me if that isn't punishment enough."

I paid the check and walked out. I left him alone at the bar, wet with urine, rigid, possibly blind and deaf. I went back to the Pink Fancy and asked them to prepare my bill. I went up to my room and called my wife. I said I'd try to get back that afternoon, but in the middle of the conversation my voice broke and I had to blow my nose.

"Don't tell me you're coming back now," she said in her sharp, high voice, using a lightly vengeful tone I had despised in the past, though at that moment it was like a balm. "Now that you're there, do me the favor of ending all this, and come back tomorrow. Did you take your pills?"

No, I hadn't taken them. With the Captain, time and my little routines had changed. I was a different man; I intended to behave like a different man. In a certain sense, I felt rejuvenated.

"Well, take them," said Gladys, "and tell him that what he did is a crime he could still be arrested for."

I hung up and lay down with my eyes wide open, staring at the ceiling. I didn't want to fall asleep because I suspected I'd feel worse afterward. So I lay there, struggling for a few minutes, until I took a mouthful of air, shook my head, and went into the bathroom. I threw up all the rum from Haiti, washed my face, and hurried to the bar to drink some coffee. Later, I went out to look for the Captain. Night had fallen on Christiansted, and I headed for the bar where I'd left him. I didn't find him there, of course, and they couldn't tell me which way he had gone. I walked around the city, and it was after eight when I stopped at the Comanche, a restaurant from the old days, and ordered soup, knowing my stomach wouldn't tolerate anything else. Then I went back to the hotel, sweating and with pains in my legs, and waited all night until dawn. At six-thirty the phone rang: they informed me that John Timothy Bunker had been taken to the hospital and had given them my name and where I could be located. They suggested I bring his underwear and toilet articles. I replied that I'd leave immediately, but I got under the blanket and tried to sleep for an hour. I needed that hour at least. It ended up being two, two hours that returned me to reality as exhausted and gloomy as I had been at the start. Devoured by remorse.

# CHAPTER SIX

ONE of the maids from the hotel came to our house to clean the kitchen, and the first thing she did was get up on a chair and begin to dust the top of the cupboard. She was humming as she dusted, and when she jumped down, her shoe flattened one of the chicks Gertrudis had given us as a gift. I was sitting on the floor, a few steps away from her; I'd just taken the chicks out of their cage and was giving them their food. The maid lifted her foot, looked at the sole of her shoe, and then looked at the little heap of feathers mixed with guts and blood. I looked too: it seemed to me something was moving, still trembling beneath the smashed flesh.

With the same rag she'd used for dusting, she picked up the chick and threw it in the trash. She implored me: "Don't tell Braulia."

I said the chicks were mine, and she replied: "Yours and Braulia's, because I've seen her feeding them too. She'll think I killed it on purpose. It'll be better if we say it got lost."

I went to the trash can to see the chick again. I was convinced she'd thrown it out while it was still alive. But all I saw were two motionless feet that were still pink. Gertrudis had told me that in time their feet turned blue.

"Lock up the others," whispered the maid. "We don't want to keep squashing them."

I didn't like her tone or the way she involved me. I left the kitchen and looked for my mother in the living room, then in her room, and finally I found her in the sewing room, sitting at the sewing machine, looking indecisively at two spools of thread that looked exactly the same color to me: burnt yellow. I went to her and said that Cecilia—that was the maid's name— had just crushed one of the chicks. For a moment she didn't know what chicks I was talking about. I had to explain that they were the ones Gertrudis had given us.

"Ah, those chicks," Mamá said with an indifferent sigh. "You shouldn't let them run around."

There was an odor of gunpowder in the air, but we hadn't heard any explosions that day. Papá had said they were going to carry out maneuvers at sea, and we'd certainly notice it the next day when the dead fish began to wash up.

"It was Cecilia's fault," I said emphatically, raising my voice, feeling a seed of rage, a livid, minuscule pellet beginning to germinate inside me, splitting open to let out its tiny shoot, which was wounding, almost carnivorous.

"It's nobody's fault, Andrés, unless it's yours. Braulia warned you to keep them in the cage."

"Cecilia jumped down without looking," I insisted vehemently, holding on to my mother's hands, those nervous hands that hadn't yet decided between two indistinguishable yellows.

"She was working," she said in a severe tone. "She wouldn't be looking out for what was on the floor."

I supposed it wouldn't be difficult for my mother to side with me, but she didn't; she said I was wrong, and I wanted to shake her, pound her with my fists, punish her in the worst way possible. A sob rose in my throat, which in a small child would have been taken simply as sniveling. Mamá raised her head, and when I looked into her eyes, it seemed to me she was a stranger. There's at least one instant in the life of a mother and child when they look and don't recognize each other; it doesn't matter how long they've lived together, or how close they appear to be. This is a moment of loss of control, of struggle, and when they confront each other it's as if they were peering into an abyss of resentment.

"I'll tell Papá you kiss the Captain," I shouted as a froth rose in my throat—nothing like sniveling, this was an adult poison. The spools of thread slipped from her hands and fell to the floor. Mamá got to her feet, stood rigid in front of me, and I noticed that only her chest was moving, rising and falling. Her breathing was all you could hear.

"What did you say, Andrés?" she asked after a few seconds, panting with fury, or emotion. At that moment I imagined she was also panting because she thought she'd been found out.

"I said the Captain kisses you and you're going to leave with him."

First I felt a slap, but Mamá was disconcerted and I was a strong boy. I didn't move my face, I didn't stop looking at her. Then she shoved me, and I did feel that. She sprang at me, her entire body against mine, and began to hit me in the face, on my head, even on my back when I turned away in an effort to dodge her. She did it in silence, choking each time she struck, suspecting that her blows couldn't hurt me and the only thing that might have shaken me had been her shove, the secret contact of her bones.

Exhausted by the effort, paler than ever, staggering as if she'd been drinking, Mamá picked up a length of cloth that had fallen to the floor, threw it haphazardly over the sewing machine, and left the room. I didn't try to see where she was going; I was afraid she was going to find my father and have the courage to tell him about my threat. It was a fear that at the same time became a hope: accusing me to Papá meant she was accusing me of lying. And that meant she had nothing to hide. I walked around the room a little, then dropped into the same chair where she'd been sewing, onto the cushion that was still warm, and I began to wait, for my father or for Braulia. I thought maybe it would be Braulia's job to come for me. But a great silence reigned throughout the house, and after a while I went back to the kitchen, like a corpse.

The cleaning woman had gone, but before she went she had placed the two chicks I'd left wandering free back into the cage. I watched them cheeping and circling each other. It occurred to me that I ought to take them out of the cage and squash them too, with my own shoe; leave them there with their guts hanging out so my mother would see them. She liked being in the kitchen so much she was bound to be the first person to discover them. I opened the cage, caught hold of one of them, put it on the floor, and raised my foot, raised it as high as I could and waited until I had the chick within range to bring down my foot. I did it forcefully, filled with an energy I'd never felt before in my life, but I missed; the chick turned and ran to hide under a table. I thought I could also catch it and put in on the meat-cutting board, and pound it down until I turned it into a soft paste. There was something I had to prevent, but I didn't know what it was or how to do it.

I wandered through an abandoned house—my mother had completely disappeared. Maybe it was then, after her argument with me, that she decided not to fight even for a minute; everything she'd been began to vanish that day, not months later when they closed her eyes. I went out to the beach, and nobody stopped me; the ocean already reeked of oil, and I stayed for a while at the edge, killing time, waiting for the bodies of marine animals though I knew it would be a while before the currents carried them to land.

When I went back to the house an hour later, I saw a car parked in front of the hotel. But my father wasn't there, he was on the balcony of the house, talking to a skinny man I thought I'd seen a few times in Isabel Segunda. I tried to walk past, but he stopped me. "Don't ask any questions and don't make any noise, understand?"

I nodded yes.

When I walked into the house, I saw Braulia sitting on the sofa, showing signs that she had been crying, though she wasn't crying just then; her gaze was distracted, and she allowed herself to be comforted by Gertrudis, who was whispering in her ear and wiping her face with a handkerchief. My mother was beside her too, squeezing one of her hands and holding a cup of some kind of tea. I stopped in front of them; Gertrudis looked at me in surprise, and Braulia seemed to wake up. I was afraid all of this had happened because of the crushed chick, a fear that grew stronger when Braulia fixed her eyes on me and burst into tears. My mother looked at me from head to toe; there was disdain in that glance, a resigned sorrow that was also a confirmation and that tore me apart inside; it hurt me much more than any blow or punishment. Papá approached, accompanied by the skinny man. "Braulia," he said, "Ramón will take you to your sister's house."

She cried even harder and stammered incomprehensible phrases. She tried to sit up by herself but gave a shriek and fell back again on the sofa in half a faint, or half crazy. I took the opportunity to reach safety; I found shelter behind the dining room table and waited there, trying to become invisible, until Braulia, who somehow had recovered, murmured words that could be heard clearly, that resonated like the verse to a song: "Santa, my poor Santa."

Mamá embraced her and whispered in her ear, and after a few minutes my father and Gertrudis helped her to stand, and with the skinny man they took her outside. I was left alone with my mother, who seemed a statue, a fierce decoration, slim and made of stone, looking at the light-filled opening through which they had gone.

I slowly approached the statue. I'm sure she detected my presence, but she didn't move, she was too wounded. I stopped beside her, stood in silence until I clearly heard the engine of the car I'd seen when I came in.

"What happened?" I asked my mother.

She didn't look at me or say a single word. She stood and walked rapidly to the kitchen, leaving me in the middle of nowhere, rigid with grief, like another statue replacing the previous one. I left the house and found myself face-to-face with my father, who was coming back in. His eyes were filled with pain, his expression was crushed, as if he'd been smashed inside, just like the chick, and there was barely a quiver left in his trampled flesh, only an illusory, utterly hopeless movement.

"What's wrong with Braulia?" I asked.

Papá thought about it; I suspect now that he was looking for the right words, but he didn't even have the energy for that.

"Her niece died. Santa was found dead this morning."

I didn't feel anything. For the moment, nothing. A mild anesthesia quieted my head, my heart, my fingers. The image of Santa looking at the autographed photograph of Urbano, the Hunger Artist, came to mind. And I recalled that, while she was looking at the photo, I'd been looking at her neckline, longing to approach, to breathe in the scent of her bosom and pick up the crumbs, the little she might want to give me, or could give me. I left the house and walked into the hotel, a ghost hotel without Gertrudis or Braulia. And without the maids, who'd gone home when they finished their work. The gardener was in Isabel Segunda, and there was no peddler in the vicinity, nobody waiting for my father or the cook to see if either one was interested in buying half a sack of yams or three dozen eggs. There was always somebody around the hotel selling things, but not that day, not then, when I'd have liked to see a human face that didn't know about the misfortune.

It was late afternoon. My father dressed to go out, and in a little while I saw that my mother had done the same. Papá had put on a mournful gray suit that made him look spectral, insomniac, or simply funereal. A dead look that fluttered in my face like the shadow of a bat. When he saw me alone, sitting in the doorway, he came toward me and said they were going to Santa's wake. If I wanted to go with them, I'd have to put on a decent shirt and trousers.

"You can wear the Zorro shirt," he advised. "But your mother doesn't want you to come. She says you insulted her."

The anesthesia began to wear off. I knew because I felt my face flushing and my hands tingling, and my heart leaped out of its passivity, beating faster than ever.

"If you're coming," Papá added, struggling inside himself, "run and get dressed."

I jumped up and ran to find the black shirt and my dress pants. I couldn't think about Santa as a dead person, and so, while I dressed, I saw her in front of me, her body naked, alive and naked, her voice asking me to touch her here or touch her there. That was all I could hear.

We drove to Matilde's house in the truck. I sat between my parents, but Mamá was obsessed with looking out the window and Papá stared straight ahead, the three of us silent, breathing in the scorched odor that was floating in the air and that smelled stronger in Isabel Segunda, an odor that mixed sometimes with the stink coming out of Montesanto, where so many of the dispossessed were sick and hundreds of animals were dying outdoors.

Long before we reached Matilde's house, we saw others heading for the wake. Papá greeted people he knew through the truck window, but Mamá put her head back and closed her eyes, as if she didn't want to see or greet anyone. I understand now that she was preparing herself to confront the sight in the coffin of a young face, grotesquely swollen and still. A short while later we got out of the truck, and I started to walk beside my father, while out of the corner of my eye I saw that Mamá lagged behind, perhaps intentionally, walking slowly, as if struggling with a force that was absorbing her against her will. When we reached Matilde's house, she crossed herself and leaned on my father's arm. Santa's body was probably in the living room, the coffin surrounded by candles and wildflowers, but there was also the enigma of death, its rancorous spirit, and my mother shuddered in anticipation of what was about to happen to us.

The men took off their hats before they went in, and through the windows you could hear the sound of crying and lamentations. Among those lamenting the loudest was Braulia. I heard her stammer some phrases and I heard her shout, and if I recognized anything in this world, even from a distance, it was the sound of her shout. After I walked through the door, I stopped. The mourners were packed so tightly you could barely walk, but my parents signaled to me to keep going, and I pushed people with my elbows and followed them. First they gave their condolences to Matilde, Santa's mother, who was sitting next to Braulia. Papá took her hand and held it for a time between his, saying words of consolation. Then it was my mother's turn, and she behaved with a certain coldness; she really didn't know Matilde very well, though perhaps it wasn't coldness but weariness, or vertigo. When she saw us, Braulia got to her feet and clung to my mother; she whispered into her ear, dampening her cheek and her gray dress. Mamá asked her to be resigned, and then Braulia insisted on taking us to see the dead girl. She began to make her way through the compact mass of mourners, and we followed her, breathing in the mixed scent of flowers, melted wax, and the smell of perspiration. Finally, I saw two women who were saying the rosary move away from the head of the coffin, and when they moved Santa's face became visible— disfigured, covered with bruises, with gray lips that weren't hers and blue-lidded eyes sunk in their sockets, lost inside the world of her skull. Braulia caressed the stiff hands clutching a small crucifix, and bent over to kiss her on the mouth. I watched the action of that kiss and felt myself being pushed against the open coffin. No one in particular was pushing me, it was all the people behind me also trying to approach. The shock of that moment changed to nausea; I felt caught, trapped between death, the brutal sleeper, and the desire to touch Santa one last time, to suck her breasts in the intimacy of the shed and roll against her entire body, her body that was dead and stinking of death, the way dogs roll in the stench of another rotting animal. Terror overwhelmed me, the emptiness of not being able to explain anything or hope for anything again. I know only that I began to shout, not crying or moving, one shout after the other, louder and louder. My father picked me up like a bundle, lifted me over the heads of the people, and took me out to the street. My voice grew silent as we moved forward, and in the darkness I felt myself becoming weak. Papá set me down at the foot of a tree, and I remained sitting there, half-intoxicated by stupefaction. Mamá came after us; she put a perfumed handkerchief under my nose and blew in my eyes. After a while she asked if I could walk; I said I could, both of them helped me to my feet, and we went back to the truck. Once again, in silence, we returned to Martineau, though this time my mother suggested that I put my head in her lap, and I did. When we got home, Papá carried me to my room, obliged me to drink a concoction Mamá had prepared to help me sleep, and undressed me as if I were a doll.

"How did Santa die?" I asked with a yawn. It was a yawn that sounded like a groan.

"They killed her, Andrés," Papá said. "But you mustn't surrender." He realized I hadn't caught the meaning of his words. "Breaking apart inside," he added, "that's surrendering."

He covered me with the sheet. I kept looking at his heavy mustache and the flutter of shadows that the lamp cast on his face.

"Who killed her?" I still wanted to know.

"Go to sleep, Andrés. You have school tomorrow."

But I hardly slept at all. I tossed and turned the whole night, and for the first time in many years, at dawn I wet the bed. As soon as it began to grow light, there was the sound of cannon and distant bursts of machine-gun fire. Planes flew over the hotel, and in a few minutes the bombardment began. That's how I knew the maneuvers were returning to dry land. Suddenly I thought of Santa, and my soul shriveled because I was never going to see her again. I squeezed my eyes shut, and when they were shut I had a premonition that the first dead fish were approaching the shore.

*THEY'RE two old photographs, small but fairly clear. Your mother gave them to me, along with the letters, and asked me to throw them into the ocean. "From the plane," she pleaded, "throw them far away." I obeyed only in part: I threw away his letters—you can't imagine the satisfaction I felt when I did that—but I decided to save the photographs. I still don't understand why. Perhaps because they were photographs of kids, children from another time, who at the moment their pictures were taken were not responsible for the life they were fated to live. I supposed that after a few years somebody, even Estela herself, would thank me for not destroying them. But your mother left this world soon afterward, and as for Frank, he never had any interest in seeing them. I mentioned them in a letter to him three or four years after he became a widower, and I confessed the truth to him: Estela had given them to me to throw in the ocean. He answered: "Then you were wrong to keep them." And we never spoke of it again.*

*The photographs were in my house on St. Croix all that time, but it never occurred to me to look at them. When my father died and I decided to move to the house I inherited in Port Clyde, I took them with me. By then I'd come back from Korea and was taking steps to bring over my wife, a Korean woman with whom I'd had a son. I began to earn my living as I'd always earned it: carrying cargo back and forth in my plane, which was no longer the Parakeet Cessna but a Piper Comanche in which I'd invested the money my father left me. When the need arose, and if I was well paid, I'd transport a corpse, one of those sleepers that* affected you so much and that, since we were in Maine, seemed colder to me and grayer, sunk deeper into their damn slumber than the sleepers in the Virgin Islands. Around that time the idea of transporting dead bodies in the plane began to make me uneasy, but unless they refused to pay what I deserved for flying with dead meat, I never said no. I didn't even need the money, I did it for the discipline, in order not to allow myself to be conquered by fear or superstition.

I never showed the photographs to my wife, or to any friend, and certainly not to my son. And one of the many reasons I didn't was that I thought nobody except you could be interested in seeing them. Before I came to see you, I looked for them; I opened the envelope where I kept them to see if they'd turned to dust, and when I found them still intact, I took them out carefully and looked at them for a long time; I bore into them with these eyes of a mortified old man who didn't do what he'd been asked to do, and then I asked myself again why I hadn't obeyed your mother, why I didn't throw them into the ocean of fifty years ago, which is not today's ocean—it's not a shadow of the ocean that used to be. I'd have given them to you last night if the cabdriver hadn't become frightened and brought me to this hospital instead of taking me to the Pink Fancy. It seems I suffered an attack; I collapsed in the taxi and became tongue-tied, and though I tried to say Pink Fancy, what came out of my mouth was a green bellowing, a muddy retching. It was partially the drink and partially my disease, the gluttonous cells I feel crawling up to my brain, like ants. It's probably a question of days before I lose the power of speech, or my mind goes blank, and when that happens, I'd like to be back in Port Clyde with my wife, who's now an old Korean woman—at our age, the fact that I'm ten years older doesn't matter very much—and my son, who's an exceptionally tall Korean because of my genes, and practically mute because of his mother's. They're very close, he and my wife, they've always communicated in a subtle way, in coded messages that nobody else could understand. That always happens with Asians.

The truth is, you have to save the photographs. It's part of the reason I came, to give you something that belongs to you; the other part was *to explain things. I must not have a very clear conscience, not for the reason you imagine, that's not it, but because of something else, a tiny doubt that may not let me die in peace, which is only a manner of speaking, after all, because who dies in peace? Imbeciles or the comatose. Nobody else. People die gasping. I've seen that dying moment too often, when everybody writhes and remembers. Remembers the past, all the windows closing, one after the other, and there's your life, like a freeze-frame in the movies. People who are seriously hurt or terminally ill always ask themselves how it will be—until you get sick you never seriously ask yourself that question—and I'm certain I know the answer. On many nights I've been able to imagine what I'm going to feel, the darkness entering through my skin, the thick ink clouding my vision. Nothing that happens then will surprise me. That's why I want you to go and get those photographs, to show you what there is in them of chance or misfortune, and to reach the end of this damn thing once and for all. You'll have to go to my room (I was so drunk I lost the key, I'll write a note and ask them to give you another one), open the suitcase, take a sealed envelope addressed to you from one of the pockets, sit down in a quiet place—I offer you my bed, my room, you can do it there—and look at them calmly. In one of the photos there are two boys: the younger one, eight or nine years old, is standing in front of a kind of wooden platform with flags on it; beside him is the older one, a boy of about fourteen, who's sitting on the ground. This one is your father; nobody has to tell you that because you'll see it on his face, it's a Syrian face, or a Lebanese one—I don't remember exactly where your grandfather came from. The younger boy is Roberto, and even back then, when the picture was taken, he had the air of hidden fervor I saw in him later. The joke is that somebody took their picture together, he and your father, who knows why, who knows where, of course on Vieques, but the photograph doesn't say the place or the occasion, only their names and the date: "Frank and Roberto, November 16, 1930."*

*The second photo is of your mother at the age of three or four, I don't think she was any older. She's leaning against the skirt of a mature woman, who's holding an infant just a few months old in her arms. Do*

*you know who the infant was? Can't you guess? Your mother told me
she and Roberto were godchildren of the same woman, the one who's in
the photograph, and so the baby who's with them is Roberto, smiling
over Estela's head, like a sign that's been throbbing ever since, like a
shadow devised to drag her down. Here, too, the joke is that their picture
was taken together, looking straight ahead at the grim future waiting for
them: dying young, almost at the same time, one of them riddled by bullets and the other willing her own death. Nothing's written on the back
of the picture. No clue, no name, no date. Your mother kept asking me
over and over to throw everything out of my plane: "Far away, please,
very far away."*

*She had less than twenty-four hours of life, and I had nothing. But
for a long time—ever since the middle of June, when the guests began to
arrive that summer, the last summer I spent with you—I'd known I'd be
left with empty hands. There was a strange activity in Frank's Guesthouse, and in your house too, an activity that seemed false to me. All the
rooms were occupied, and visitors were constantly arriving, people staying in hotels in Isabel Segunda who'd come to your hotel with the flim-
siest excuses: they were going to look around, or visit other guests, or
have a drink at the little bar your father had set up on the beach, under
a canopy of palm leaves. I don't know if you realized it, because you
were a boy, but a moment came when you couldn't tell the guests from
the conspirators. American guests mixed in the dining room with intractable nationalists like the barber and the barber's friends, who were
passing through Isabel Segunda, looking at everything as if they were
Martians and arousing who knows how many suspicions. I'm sure they
were being watched. Roberto remained apart, as silent as always, and
spent hours behind closed doors with your father. Estela was so happy to
have him there that she went around filled with vitality, barely hiding
her nervousness, excited down to her bones. I knew because I came to
Martineau and asked for my usual room. I intended to spend more time
at the hotel, and I almost never went out; I pretended to read a book
about aviation and pretended I was resting, but my mind found no rest.*

*You moved around in the middle of the whirlwind; you hit it off*

*with the barber, or he tried to hit it off with you, and since you were vul-
nerable, longing to find a support, still shaken by the death of that girl,
you let yourself be won over with no problem. The barber knew how to
listen to you, I believe he had a boy your age, and at one point he improvised a little barbershop in the storeroom of the hotel and asked you
to be his assistant. He put a chair in there and began to cut the hair of
everybody who didn't want to go to the barbershops in Isabel Segunda,
which at that time were always filled with Marines. I had fairly short
hair, and my own barber on St. Croix, so it didn't occur to me to request
his services, but Roberto did—he had thick, full hair, the kind of mane
where it's very easy to imagine a woman's fingers.*

*One morning, when I passed by the improvised barbershop, I saw
your father there reading the paper, and your mother listening to the
news on a small radio they'd placed on the table where the barber had set
up his shaving soap and razor. Roberto was in the chair, letting himself
be sheared, or that's what it looked like given the amount of hair falling
to the floor. I stopped in the doorway, and your mother looked up and
raised her eyebrows as if she was surprised to see me, while your father
simply gestured with his hand, inviting me in. The barber interrupted
his work for a moment and looked at me with a dubious expression—I
couldn't tell if it was distrust or defiance. Roberto didn't even bother to
look at me; he didn't shift his gaze, he kept his eyes fixed on the wall
in front of him, a bare wall except for a ridiculous calendar. I saw him in
profile; he had a straight nose and a hard chin, an unbreakable look on
his sullen face. I didn't know whether to keep going or to stay with them
and try to start a conversation. But at heart I felt excluded, and that ex-
clusion seemed like an insult to me. I had helped them with weapons;
I'd carried their pistols in my own plane, and the submachine gun the barber used later to defend himself. I'd risked my hide when we left Vieques
in the launch on New Year's Day, and risked it again when we reached the
port of Fajardo and unloaded the crates of fish (which in reality were crates
of pistols) and put them in a truck that took off at top speed for San Juan.
I don't know if your father felt uncomfortable; all he said was: "Come in,
J.T., did you want a haircut?" and I shook my head.*

*I turned and headed for the beach, and on the way I ran into Brau-*
*lia, carrying a tray filled with cups of coffee. She stopped to offer me one,*
*and I'll bet she saw the resentment and indignation in my eyes. Who*
*knows what the hell she saw, because it seemed to me she softened, tried*
*to show her more accommodating side, or her sweeter side, which was an*
*impossible side. The only person who knew, or suspected, what had*
*happened between your mother and me was Braulia. And at that mo-*
*ment she was the only one who realized I was behaving like a dog, a*
*lapdog, humiliating myself in order to get back with Estela. Braulia*
*knew—which meant her friend the dyke knew too—that I was stung by*
*Roberto's presence, but my hands were tied out of respect for your father.*
*I never knew if Estela was open with her. At times I think your mother*
*was never open with anybody, never told her true feelings to another per-*
*son. Not her sister, her friends, not even Braulia, who knew what*
*everybody in that house was feeling, and knew perfectly well that Frank*
*was involved in the nationalist conspiracy and Estela was an accessory,*
*in a sense a kind of connection and also a point of reference for the group*
*led by the barber, who pretended to be an idiot with his scissors but ac-*
*tually was a very clever man, with a courage no one could have imag-*
*ined until he barricaded himself in his barbershop.*

*You were absolutely mistaken, Andrés. You were always mistaken,*
*and fifty years ago it was forgivable because you were a child, but now I*
*can't believe you're still insisting on something you surely saw in dreams,*
*or saw some other way, or wanted to see but it never happened; that day*
*didn't exist on any calendar in the world. You smelled the danger, that's*
*true, but the attitude of your mother, who was subtle, disoriented you,*
*and the attitude of Roberto, who was a block of silence, an unassailable*
*being, left no room for suspicions. Perhaps that was what hurt me most:*
*your mother didn't realize, except toward the end, that the man had only*
*one attachment, one desire in his life, and that was the struggle. Under-*
*stand, it was a different time, and we were different people. Though*
*maybe I shouldn't include myself because I'm still the same, and even in*
*1950 I was exactly like I am now: it's a question of character. I never*
*felt his conviction or devotion. Compared to Roberto, I must have seemed*

*a colorless creature; I suspected it then and see it clearly now. If I'd been a woman, I'd have chosen him too, the man who didn't want to choose anybody, who wasn't available except for what he said: proclaiming independence, shouting Republic, and getting all of us out of there, getting rid of the gringos as if they were roaches, and getting the hell rid of me.*

*Go to the Pink Fancy. Tell them I'm in the hospital and lost my key but that you have to pick up my things. I beg you, don't go to sleep tonight without seeing those photographs. Blow on them, as if they were dusty, and you'll see that in fact an unreal cloud of dust lifts and the secret appears. Tomorrow, before you catch your flight to San Juan, you ought to come and see me. I promise you it will be the last time; we're the only survivors, and somebody has to speak. I'll do it. I'll begin where it hurts us most.*

# CHAPTER SEVEN

IT was a silent, tense summer. As if everyone, including the guests, was wandering around inside a separate cloud, sleepwalkers in the grit. The barber came to spend a few days with us, and two other men, who were his friends and also friends of my father, came with him and stayed in the same room. None of them brought his wife or children, which would have been the logical thing to do since we were on vacation. They got together in the afternoons to talk, and sometimes they walked along the beach, two by two, smoking and looking at the waves. During this time, another friend of the family dropped by the hotel: it was Roberto, and since there were no empty rooms left, Papá invited him to stay in our house, in the same room where we'd held the Christmas Eve vigil for the dead man who hanged himself. No one had slept in the bed since then, and my mother gave orders to turn the mattress, make it up with clean sheets— which she took from the drawers of her bureau herself—and to put the fine washstand and mirror that had belonged to Apolonia in the room. One of the maids brought towels from the hotel, but my mother took them out and replaced them with the soft towels that were used only in the house. I'll bet the man didn't even realize all the trouble that had been taken to make him feel comfortable. Certainly he must have thought the room was always like that, elegant and filled with nice touches, like the rooms in magazines. And even though he was in the house for several days, he never ate breakfast with us; he'd get up at dawn and have breakfast in the hotel dining room with the barber Vidal and his friends.

One morning, one of the guests, an elderly American with a patch over one eye like a pirate (he'd lost it in the First World War), asked Papá to take him to the barbershop in Isabel Segunda. Papá, who probably didn't have the time or desire to take him in the truck, said there was a barber in the hotel in case he'd like to have his shave there. That was how Braulia prepared the storeroom where we kept tools and cans of paint and turned it into Vidal's barbershop, and all the guests wanted haircuts and shaves, and even the peddlers who came out to Martineau to sell their wares took out a few coins when they heard a barber was at work there, and Vidal charged them less money, or sometimes he didn't charge them money at all but took vegetables they'd brought for the kitchen as payment.

Only one woman came to the place to have her hair cut: it was Gertrudis. Vidal had asked me to be his assistant, and when Gertrudis came in, a little before lunchtime, wearing her black skirt and white blouse, and asked if he could take care of her, the barber held her gaze and said he'd be happy to and how could he serve the señora. He said it with a touch of irony, rather ceremoniously—I don't know if he expected Gertrudis to say she wanted a shave—and she didn't crack a smile. She opened the collar of her blouse and sat in the chair, which was an ordinary chair with cushions so that the customers would sit at a certain height and the barber could work comfortably. Braulia stopped in the doorway and gave her friend an understanding look; you could see the electricity between them, a current of virile tenderness. Vidal cut mercilessly; very professional and working in silence, he didn't exchange a single word with his client, perhaps because he realized that Gertrudis had no interest in exchanging even half a word with him. As soon as I could, I went to find my mother so she could come and see the show, and I found her pruning the plants in the courtyard, talking to the Captain, who'd come to the hotel for a few days and was staying in his usual room. I was happy to interrupt them, to interpose myself in their conversation as they stood close to each other. J.T. was smoking a cigarette, his dark panama pulled down to his eyebrows, and my mother was bending over the plants of everlasting, cutting and at the same time examining some leaves that seemed unhealthy. The Captain raised his freckled face; it looked troubled to me, or maybe he found the sun devastating. I avoided looking at him but went up to my mother and whispered that the barber was cutting Gertrudis's hair. My mother smiled; it was a smile of complicity directed not at me but at the Captain, who pushed his hat back and revealed his entire face, as if he were revealing his true intentions.

"It must be the worms," my mother complained, turning back to the sickly leaves. And then, as if she realized I was waiting for her, she extended her hand and touched my arm. "Go back to the barber. I'll come later."

I understood that she wanted me to leave. The Captain's expression did not change; he only looked at the ground, pretending he didn't care about anything. I insisted, I begged my mother to please come with me, but she replied that Gertrudis might get annoyed, and maybe the barber would too, if he realized we weren't taking his work seriously. I didn't answer but stood there hesitating, not daring to take a step. My mother realized that all I wanted was to separate her from J.T., which apparently was enough to make her stubborn: she turned her back on me and went on with what she was doing, pruning plants, poking at each leaf in search of the worms. I don't know how much time went by, one minute or five, until the Captain decided to break the ice: "Come on, Andrés, I'll go with you."

I looked at Mamá to see if she was sorry, if she hated me because I'd finally succeeded in separating them. And Mamá shuddered, even from the back I could see her shudder, as if my gaze,

a needle of ice, passed right through her body. I returned to the
hotel with the Captain, and we went to the storeroom, where
the barber was finishing up with Gertrudis. She gave us a savage
look and didn't even greet the Captain. The barber handed her
a mirror so she could see the cut, and Gertrudis, facing the mirror, shook her head like an entirely satisfied horse. She paid,
mumbled "So long," and I suppose she went to the beach, since
you could see the straps of her bathing suit under her shirt. All
this happened on July 3. I remember because the next day, a holiday when fireworks had been scheduled in Isabel Segunda, we
had a strange visitor at the hotel. A slim, dark-skinned woman
with very restless green eyes and a small, red-painted mouth that
looked like a miniature heart came to the hotel and asked for my
mother. Braulia greeted her, asked her to have a seat in the re-
ception area, and then went to the barbershop to find me. "Go
tell your mother a lady's here who wants to see her. I think she's
from St. Croix."

I went out and saw the woman, sitting very stiffly, though
she moved her eyes from one side to the other, examining
everything. She wore medium-heeled shoes and a striped dress,
but the showiest item was her hat, made of natural straw, with
multicolored flowers attached to the black band. I ran to the
house, and when I found my mother, I realized Braulia hadn't
told me the name of the woman who wanted to see her, so all I
said was that a lady from St. Croix was waiting for her in the hotel. She was sewing and hurt herself with the needle; she lifted
her finger to her mouth and looked up, and I sensed her fear.

"From St. Croix, are you sure?"

I told her I was but didn't wait for her because I was more
interested in the haircutting lesson the barber was giving me.
When Braulia had interrupted us, he was teaching me how to
hold the comb and cut the hair on a diagonal, from bottom to
top. And so I ran back to the barbershop, but when I got there
Vidal was listening to the radio, and he signaled for me to be

quiet. Minutes later one of the men who had traveled with him from San Juan came in. He was wearing a three-piece suit and dark tie, as if he weren't in a hotel on the beach. Vidal, who was in a squat with his ear to the radio, got to his feet when he saw him. "They just fucked Korea."

He bent down again, but I noticed he wasn't paying attention to what the announcer was saying. His mind was somewhere else, his eyes fixed on the floor.

"On top of that," he said, his voice dragging, "Truman signed Law 600. So we've just been fucked too."

Neither of them seemed to remember I was there. The barber moved around the room, looked everywhere, including the ceiling, as if he suddenly had been dropped there and was searching for an opening to slip through.

"Let Roberto know we're going to meet," he told his friend, "and tell Ríos to find the people from Isabel Segunda."

He turned off the radio and sat down in the chair that had been improvised for his customers. He looked at his hands, which moisture had turned pink, lighter than the rest of his body. I realized he had ordinary, fairly small hands, which perhaps was the reason he was dexterous with the scissors. I picked up the can of talc and moved it from one place to another; I made a small noise intended to attract his attention. He didn't even bother to look at me, but even so I asked him where Korea was.

"Next to China," he murmured, thinking about something else, "between the Yellow Sea and the Sea of Japan."

I sprinkled talc in my hand and brought it up to the back of my neck. I rubbed slowly, I can't remember to what end.

"There's going to be a war," the barber said. "They'll take the boys from here and from Isla Grande. They'll kill them in Korea, or they'll come back with only one leg or one arm. And the ones who don't die will have to kill Koreans."

I thought it was a thousand times better to kill Koreans than to come back without legs. I thought it but didn't say it because just then the barber stood up and said he had to go see his friends and would keep teaching me how to cut hair when he had another chance.

"Tomorrow?" I insisted.

"Tomorrow," he agreed.

I walked out of the hotel, and in the distance I saw the woman who'd come to see my mother—that is, I saw her striped dress—and I knew she'd just left my house. She saw me too and stopped, changed direction, and began to walk toward me. I imagined she'd go back into the hotel or ask me to find Braulia. But when she was beside me, she leaned over a little, put her face at the level of mine, and breathed these words: "Your mother's going away."

She exaggerated the movement of her lips, as if she were speaking to a deaf person. I didn't know what to say or how to escape. Our faces were very close, and since she was breathing rapidly, I could smell the odor of her mouth, which wasn't bad or good, just that odor peculiar to each person, the odor of one's teeth, or tongue, or throat. I turned around looking for support, Braulia's help or the help of the maids, but I didn't see anybody. She realized this and moved away from me. Then she fixed her eyes on the hotel. "She's going away and leaving all of you," she said emphatically, clutching at a black handbag. "Tell your father."

I watched her walk away toward the highway and supposed that a cab, or some kind of vehicle, was waiting for her there. Nobody could come to Martineau on foot, or walk anywhere else. I went in the house. I knew my father was in Isabel Segunda, or maybe picking up fish in La Esperanza. I looked for my mother in the sewing room, I looked for her in the kitchen, and finally I found her in her room, sitting on the edge of the bed.

"Wash your hands," she ordered without looking at me, "I'm ready to serve lunch."

She seemed preoccupied, and I waited in vain for her to tell me about the woman who'd just left, who she was or why she had come. I was about to ask her, or to repeat what the woman had said to me. But I decided it was better for me to go to the bathroom and begin soaping my hands. I spent long minutes turning the suds around until I couldn't see them anymore because my eyes blurred, and what I saw was a ball of mist, all my fingers transformed into fog that became more distant and more dense. I rinsed my hands and splashed water on my face. I went down to the dining room and sat at the table. Nobody came—not a sign of my mother with lunch, not a sound, not a word from her. The minutes went by, and I was afraid to go looking for her or to call her or even to move in the chair. After a while I heard her come down; I saw her pass by me and go into the kitchen.

"Come help me," I heard her say, and I understood that her tone was serious.

My eyes were burning, and my legs were trembling a little. She put a bowl of white rice in my hands. "Take this to the table."

I carried in the rice and came back to help some more. My mother looked at me in dismay, not knowing what to do with me. She told me to take in the platter of salad, the slices of avocado that looked like sarcastic green smiles. She picked up the bowl of red beans. We walked as if it were a procession, and we put everything on the table. I knew Mamá wanted to cry; the desire to cry can be seen most forcefully in the way people walk. We ate by ourselves, in silence. My mother made some ambiguous remark about the lessons the barber was giving me. She suggested that later I could practice shaving Gerónimo, for instance, or give haircuts to Elodio Brito, the hotel cook. I didn't answer. She stood, picked up the empty dishes, and went back to the kitchen.

My father came home in the middle of the afternoon. He looked for me around the house and found me on the beach. I'd been swimming and was resting on the sand, watching Gertrudis, who swam with long strokes in the distance, not wearing her orange bathing cap because, with her hair so short, she didn't need to put it on. I didn't realize Papá was there until I looked to the side and saw the tips of his two-toned shoes.

"We'll go to Isabel Segunda," he announced. "Don't you want to see the fireworks?"

We were alone, or almost alone. There were a few guests nearby: the old man with the eye patch, and his wife, both of them sprawling on the sand, sizzling in the sun like chameleons. And a young couple, Americans as well, but the wife had an Asian look; she was asleep on her towel, her skin the color of bread crusts and her breasts pointing at the sky, like a motionless doll that reminded me of Santa, which was why it hurt me to look at her. I hesitated between telling Papá about my mother's visitor and keeping silent.

"We leave at seven sharp," he added, "so don't stay here too long."

I wanted to ask if Mamá would come with us. I was afraid that, with both of us away, she'd leave without any explanations, not saying goodbye, maybe leaving us a letter. In the soap operas she listened to on the radio, people were always leaving a letter to say goodbye. I knew because sometimes I listened to them with her. I began digging in the sand, thinking about that, looking out of the corner of my eye at my father, who was walking quickly back to the hotel. At that moment the girl who reminded me of Santa woke up, stretched on her towel, and whispered something to her husband. They both got to their feet, and she adjusted her bathing suit, which was black and, while she was sleeping, had pulled up over her buttocks, leaving them slightly exposed. I thought of Santa's buttocks, which I hadn't seen very often but had touched, briefly, when I embraced her. They were hard buttocks, always a little cold. I stood up to go back to the house. My head was burning, and for a fraction of a second, only a fraction, I saw the image of my mother naked, and the Captain, without his shirt but wearing a hat, hugging her at the edge of the water.

I went to my room, took a shower, and washed off the sand and salt water. Just as my father had said, at seven sharp we left for Isabel Segunda. I knew that some guests were already in town and that J.T. would join us a little later because he had to fly that day to St. Croix. My parents talked about it in the truck, and only then did I understand Mamá's reasons for wanting to go with us, so absorbed in her sadness but at the same time so iron-willed, planning to see him.

On the square in Isabel Segunda there was music, stands selling fried food, and crowds of the dispossessed, some of them barefoot, walking back and forth to see what might come their way, somebody who'd take pity on them and buy them a piece of meat or a shot of rum because we were celebrating American Independence Day. Most of the Marines were not wearing uniforms, but in spite of their clothing you could see who they were. Papá said hello to his friends from town, and my mother also stopped to kiss her former classmates or some fluttering old ladies who identified themselves as friends of my grandmother. The barber and his men were waiting for us along the road, on the slope that leads to Fort Count Mirasol, from whose esplanade we were going to watch the fireworks. Right after we started to climb the hill, we ran into them. Papá said hello as if he were surprised to see them; they talked for a few minutes, and then we continued walking together. Or almost together, since the barber lagged behind, and I noticed right away that he was doing it intentionally. From time to time I turned my head to be sure he was behind me, and he winked at me, to which I responded with another wink, hoping that the Captain wouldn't appear, that he'd stay on St. Croix or crash into the ocean in his plane. As we climbed, Mamá put her arm around my shoulders, and suddenly I shivered.

When we reached the fort, we gathered at the highest spot and waited almost an hour until we heard the first explosions and saw the first lights. My father was watching next to the barber, and my mother and I kept very close, staring at the sky, probably feeling the same uneasiness, looking for a sign. Once when I turned my head to say something to my father, I realized that Roberto, that friend of his, had just arrived, or perhaps he'd been there from the beginning and I'd only just noticed his presence. The entire group conversed without looking at anybody else, as if they were talking to themselves, not missing a detail of the fireworks, all of them enthralled, their eyes shining. At the end there was an enormous explosion—it was difficult to follow the trajectory of so many lights—and shouts of amazement and the sound of little children crying. Before the smoke cleared, Papá came over to us and said the best thing would be for us to go home. Mamá didn't say anything but took my arm, and we headed for the road that ended at the dock, where we'd left the truck. Other people were walking beside us, but not my father's friends, who surely had remained at the fort. But other people's conversations didn't touch us. We were filled with a peculiar silence, a silence that signified unspeakable things.

When the three of us were in the truck, and my father had already started the engine, a woman came up to the window and said my mother's name. She did it with some timidity, as if she weren't very sure she'd be recognized. Mamá reacted with joy, got out again, and embraced the woman. They began to ask each other about their respective sisters and children, and I looked at my father; it was urgent I look at him. Papá felt it, I believe my eyes bore into his temple, and still I kept looking at him: at his profile and the lock of hair that fell onto his high, preoccupied forehead.

"Mamá's going away," I whispered, torn apart by worry.

"No," my father replied, "she's only saying hello to a friend."

"She'll go away with the Captain," I whispered to him again in a thin voice. His lips trembled, and he swallowed but didn't look at me. "A woman who was in Martineau today told me to tell you that Mamá would go away." He kept staring straight ahead. Not a single muscle moved in his face. We listened to the conversation between my mother and her friend; they were talking about the hotel, about the soot everywhere after the maneuvers, about the noise of the explosions. "Papá," I begged, "Papá . . ."

They were saying goodbye. My mother's friend wrote her address on a piece of paper so we could visit her the next time we went to San Juan. There, in the darkness of the truck, feeling my father's pained breathing, his stony silence, the heat coming out of his body, a rough heat filled with powerlessness, I was certain we'd never go back to Isla Grande. We'd never go back to my aunt's house, or take a walk through the Barrio Obrero. I'd never again see the eyes of Urbano, the weak eyes of that artist of desolation.

"J.T.'s going to take her away."

I saw Papá dig his nails into the steering wheel. I never called the Captain of the Sleepers J.T. I did it then as a desperate measure, perhaps my last chance to provoke my father and force him to react.

Mamá got back in the truck with a smile on her lips. She said something about her friend's husband and looked again at the scrap of paper with her address before putting it away in her handbag. Papá didn't say a word during the ride back, and my mother and I didn't open our mouths again either. We were like three strangers passing through an internal night, more intractable and blacker than the one surrounding us.

I went back to the Pink Fancy, explained that John Timothy Bunker was in the hospital, and gave them his handwritten note authorizing me to pick up his belongings. I accepted the key to his room but didn't go in right away; I wanted to wait awhile, and I went to the bar. I ordered a vodka martini, and as I was sipping it I tried to remember what mattered to me most: my father's appearance in June 1973, the last time we saw each other, a few days before his death. At that time he was living in a little town in Georgia called Milledgeville, with his American wife and her daughter, who was retarded. Papá was dying of lupus, and he looked very weak; he spoke in whispers and had lost his usual color, which was an olive color. He was not yet sixty, but the disease had dried him out, sucked in his cheeks, and affected his voice.

My father's wife received me in tears; she thanked me for coming to Georgia, because Frankie (she called him Frankie) was always asking for me. Her daughter also received me with a weepy face, though she immediately began to smile, and wearing that empty smile, she shook my hand. A short while later the two women accompanied me to the room where my father was sleeping. Helen, his wife, brought in a chair, placed it next to the bed, and asked me to sit down. During all this time Papá was snoring and didn't even wake at the sound of our conversation. His wife had to call to him, stretching out her plump hand and touching him gently on the cheek. "Frankie, look who's here. District Attorney Yasín has come to see you."

She said this without irony, then added that my father always referred to me that way. He half-opened his eyes and looked in a distracted way at his wife and stepdaughter, who did not stop smiling. Then he looked in the opposite direction and saw me there; I believe he also saw the part of him that was in my eyes, my nose, my mouth that was identical to his. I was almost thirty-five at the time, his age when our misfortune occurred. I leaned over the bed and kissed his cheek; his wife asked if we'd like some iced tea, and Papá answered for both of us: with the tatters of his old voice he told her to bring the tea. She took her daughter's arm and led her away over the protests of the girl, who was of indeterminate age and whose milky flesh gave the impression of also being liquid and cold. When we were alone, Papá insisted on what he'd said to me on the phone the week before: it was foolish to pay for a hotel room when they had a guest room in the house. I defended myself with a phrase that to his ears must have sounded like distant flattery: "I like sleeping in small hotels."

He smiled in a melancholy way and immediately made the gesture of someone chasing away an evil thought, a dark, laughable temptation. He asked about my job, and I said it was barely three months since my appointment as district attorney. I missed private practice and was still getting used to calls in the middle of the night to go to a crime scene. He made a move to sit up, and I went to help him, propped him up on pillows, and felt the ignominy of his bones, his wasted limbs, the acrid smell coming from his skin. With some embarrassment, he mentioned that the disease fluctuated and this was the worst crisis he'd suffered.

"Maybe it's the last," he added with feigned casualness. "I can't stand."

There were two photographs on the night table. One of him with his wife, celebrating an anniversary to judge by the corsage she wore at her neckline. And the other of him and me, the day of my graduation, a photograph full of light, taken in the gardens of Columbia University. He caught me looking at them and mumbled something unusual in a man like him who had always avoided the principal topic of our lives.

"We were still looking a little dead."

It was true. We were both making an effort to smile, as if we'd been forced to stand next to those hedges, in that immense light, with him in a suit and me in my graduation robe, both of us afflicted and in a certain sense indifferent.

"I have some pictures for you." He pointed feebly at the bureau. "Wait for Helen to come back and she'll give them to you."

Helen appeared a short while later with two glasses of tea. Her daughter stayed in the doorway, not daring to come in but looking at me constantly. Papá smiled at her from the bed, as if he were looking at a little girl, and he explained that the girl thought I was her brother.

"She doesn't know what the word *brother* means. But when she sees your photograph, she says that's what you are."

My father's wife looked at me in some embarrassment; it seemed to me she felt the need to apologize. Papá realized this and changed the subject; he asked her to get the photographs, she knew which ones. Helen smiled in gratitude and opened a drawer: the envelope was on top, waiting for me. I took it with a certain disenchantment and put it on my knees.

"Open it." My father's voice trembled.

They were all photographs of my childhood. Most of them on the beach, with the guests, or with Braulia, or in the company of my mother. In one I picked up at random, I suddenly saw myself with the Captain. It was a picture dated 1949, taken at the edge of the ocean. J.T. was wearing shorts with an oval design, and his hair looked dark brown because in photographs you couldn't distinguish red. I calculated that twenty-four years had gone by since the day I saw him for the last time. I'd grown up and studied the law, gone to Vietnam, married, had a five-year-old son. But I felt ashamed and set the picture aside, hiding it quickly so Papá wouldn't see, not thinking that he was the very one who'd put it there, with the others, intending for me to keep it.

"There's one of your birthday," he rambled in a low voice. "I'm not sure if it was your birthday or Estela's."

It was mine. I knew as soon as I saw the photograph, the desolation in my father's face and the unwilling expression in my own eyes, my tight, sad mouth. Mamá was at a distance, wearing a grimace of resignation, grief, or guilt. I looked at her, trying to understand, but I didn't want to linger over her. We kept the pictures, I thanked Helen, and I heard the bellow that came out of her daughter's throat, a bellow of approval or of impatience, it was impossible to determine about what.

I was alone again with my father. It was the second time I had visited him in his house in Georgia. After my graduation we didn't see each other very much, and he was almost always the one who traveled to San Juan. We'd write to each other but never touched on the topic of the Captain, much less my mother's end. Perhaps some trivial allusion, nothing that would oblige us to go on talking. And not even during this visit, as conscious as he was that he had very little time left, did he want us to lay our cards on the table. The only thing he consistently talked to me about during the hours we spent together was himself, his childhood in Isabel Segunda and the nationalist fervor of Apolonia, his mother, who used the bands of the flag to teach him the names of colors when he was a child. When he was five or six years old, my father would ask when he was going to see his father Khalil, and Apolonia, who didn't know when the wandering Lebanese would show up, told him the truth: she couldn't say, because he always arrived when least expected, when it suited him to pass through Vieques on his way to St. Croix, or when some client in Isabel Segunda sent for him. But to keep him from thinking too much about Khalil, Apolonia told him the story of White Eagle, her revolutionary lover from 1898, and showed him a picture of the man, an old hand-tinted photograph that, with the passage of time, in her years of senile madness, she herself mislaid. Apolonia, according to Papá, had been a political animal her entire life, perhaps because her own father, my great-grandfather, had been a founding member of the League of Patriots and would hold its pro-independence meetings in the guesthouse in Isabel Segunda, the same one my grandmother later inherited.

"One day she took me to the dock in Punta Arenas," Papá recalled and held out his hand, dreaming about Apolonia's hand. "She told me we were going to meet someone important, and I thought it was Khalil (sometimes she called him Khalil, and sometimes Papá Khalil, never just Papá), and so I was happy, but Mamá didn't know."

"Mothers never know," I murmured, in so lugubrious a tone my father gave a start, as if only at that moment, in that bed, in that town so far from the place where we belonged, he'd seen that his son still felt the pangs of rancor.

"It's just that her head was in the clouds," he added, excusing my grandmother. "Pedro Albizu Campos was coming to Vieques to meet with nationalist women; it was the first time they'd organized into an assembly. They hadn't done that even on Isla Grande. And Apolonia was the first one at the dock, the first to receive him, with me at her side, and I was disappointed to discover it wasn't Khalil who was coming but another Lebanese. Albizu looked like a real Moor."

He tried to laugh and couldn't. He started to choke and looked at me with fear. In that fear I saw his desire to say everything, to spew up everything and then die.

"It was the middle of November, and it was drizzling. He came down from the launch and stood looking at the group of women waiting for him. Some had brought their young children.

I was fourteen and grown up, I felt grown up, but Roberto—do you remember him?—was a boy of seven or eight, and he came down to the dock with his godmother because he was an orphan. Albizu called to him and touched his head. That touch was enough. Nationalism got inside his skull."

After each sentence Papá licked his lips. I saw that his tongue was pale and dry, already covered with thick saliva, the saliva of the dying.

"He spent two nights in Isabel Segunda, one of them in your grandmother's guesthouse. On Saturday they held their ceremonies in the public square, and the assembly took place on Sunday in the theater. Outside the theater they took a picture of Roberto and me; I kept it for a long time, but then your mother got hold of it and I don't know where she put it. On the night that Albizu spent with us, Apolonia couldn't sleep a wink. She walked around, went to his room to see if he needed anything, and when she found him asleep, called me so I could see him. There was little to see, after all: an unmoving man in striped pajamas. Many years later, when your grandmother was already dead, I told Albizu what we'd done: spied on him while he was sleeping. He attributed no importance to it and said maybe that was the reason I was on his side, because I'd seen him stripped of consciousness in the world where all men are equal, the world of the sleepers."

My father finished speaking and sank into a kind of stupor. His wife told me this often happened to him because he was weak. That night, in the little hotel in Milledgeville, I looked at the photographs again, lingering over all of them but especially the one in which the Captain and I were together. I scrutinized his eyes, which were almost inscrutable, and I stared at his body, muscular but with a fair amount of fat around the waist: he had a solid, vulgar belly. And against the belly, I thought, more the result of self-assurance than of overeating, he'd pressed the smooth stomach of my mother. Against that belly she surely had rested her head and dozed. I was imagining them like that, satisfied and lazy, though it made me miserable to imagine them.

The next day, when I went back to his house, Papá insisted on talking to me about the nationalists' reasons for moving forward the date of the uprising. He recounted in detail what he'd already said in other conversations we'd had at different times: except for him, and a few others that no one ever suspected, the men had been watched day and night, and then the police seized a car with pistols and ammunition that belonged to them. Either they began the revolution right away or they'd all go to jail without having the chance to fire a single shot or to lift a finger against Law 600, a "deceptive thing," as Albizu said, because it paved the way for a constitution that would never allow them to be free.

"We failed," Papá said sadly. "I hope Apolonia has forgiven me, because we began like madmen. It was madness from beginning to end, and then the world was all over us. The world was the FBI, the police, the national guard. They crushed us and wiped us out. They considered us dead, and dead we remained."

Helen, my father's wife, cooked a big lunch. It was the last time Papá got out of bed, and even though he was very pale, he stayed at the table until we finished. Later, back in his room, he asked if I ever happened to see the barber.

"Vidal died," I said.

"Of course," he acknowledged. "He died of it, didn't he? Forgive me, I'm confused. It's the pills."

But I know he was perfectly lucid when he asked if I'd run into the Captain again.

"J.T. helped us at first," he continued, as if he really didn't care very much about my answer. "He did it out of friendship for me. And he didn't betray us, as Estela thought. If he had, they'd have arrested me then and I wouldn't be here today, dying of this damn lupus."

He said "damn lupus" with disdain, showing me his scaly arms riddled with needle marks. Before I left the house I promised him I'd be back in two weeks. But I didn't go back in two weeks, or three, and in the fourth week he died. He'd arranged to be buried in the little town of Milledgeville, where I returned just in time to lead the funeral procession to the cemetery. My father's wife seemed exhausted and didn't cry. Her daughter, by contrast, wailed and shouted when they began to lower the coffin. Later there was a buffet—a real American funeral—which several of my father's friends attended. After selling the hotel, Papá had earned his living in real estate until lupus took him out of the race. Among the men whom I didn't know but who had been his colleagues was a monumental old man with a gray beard and green eyeglasses; he attracted my attention when I saw him in the cemetery, and later, at the buffet, he stood beside me at the table as we served ourselves chicken salad. Then he took a vial out of his pocket and sprinkled something on his plate. When he glanced up, he caught me looking at him. "Mustard seed," he declared in a voice of clattering stones that seemed to come from his stomach. "What happens after death is always a confirmation."

Everything came together and exploded in my body. My bones and teeth hurt, and I walked to the hall, looking for my father's room. I pushed open the door and sat down on the bed that still held his final traces. I wept quietly, alone, for several minutes. I unburdened myself and then went back to the living room. The man with the mustard seeds had already left, and the widow's daughter came up to me and looked into my eyes. I'm sure she understood I'd been crying, because she lifted her hand and with clumsy fingers touched my cheeks. She did it as if she were drying invisible tears, as if her imbecility had vanished for a moment. She didn't smile, and neither did I. I had a feeling a miracle was taking place at that moment, the result of a death, my father's death. And the miracle was the illogical confirmation that the past was still alive.

# CHAPTER EIGHT

I turned twelve in September. Papá gave me a book: *Moby-Dick*. Mamá hadn't gone away, and that may have been her best present, but she also got me a pair of sunglasses I had asked her for a while ago. Braulia prepared a cake with blue icing, and the maids blew up balloons and hung paper chains in the hotel lobby. My friends from school came, nine or ten kids with their parents. Among them was a skinny boy with a consumptive's dark circles under his eyes, who brought me a baseball as a gift. He put it in my hands and looked at me with hatred. Later, when our mothers moved away to talk, he ran over to me to take it and hide it in one of his pockets. Nobody was aware of his actions, and a simple shove on my part would have been enough to stop him from taking it—that boy was like a feather—but I didn't care.

J.T. also came, almost at the end of the afternoon. He'd just arrived from St. Croix, disheveled and even a little dirty. He always looked very tired when he came in from flying, but that day he also seemed drowsy and short-tempered. He gave the impression that he was there more to settle accounts with us or to fight about something than to celebrate a birthday. He said he had a present for me and gave me a stuffed purple fish that looked like a miniature dirigible bristling with barbs. He told me it was a poisonous species that inflated when it was going to shoot its venom. I looked for the fish's eyes and found two little black beads set under the largest barbs, which resembled a pair of horns on its head. I asked the Captain if they were real eyes, and he said no, because eyes couldn't be preserved. It was a fairly cold conversation on both our parts, and as we talked I noticed that he smelled of sweat and also gave off an intense odor of liquor. I understand now that he drank when he was flying. He often turned on the radio and listened to baseball games as he flew from one island to another in his overloaded plane, swallowing mouthfuls of whiskey. Papá once remarked that J.T. always overloaded his plane.

"I saw submarines," he announced that day. "They're easy to see from a height."

It may have been a baited hook. But if it was, I swallowed it right away. I asked the Captain if we could go up in his plane to see the submarines. We were celebrating my birthday, and I knew Papá wouldn't say no. And my mother even less so because it had to do with J.T., and everything done with him, or for him, had her blessing. They were different times, and flying wasn't as common as it is now, but in my family those short flights were considered ordinary. For us it was faster and easier to get into J.T.'s plane than to travel to Punta Arenas and catch the passenger launch that made the trip to Isla Grande. The Captain agreed we'd go the next day on what he called a "reconnaissance flight." I asked if the submarines would still be there.

"They're always there," Papá said with a smile. "Don't worry about that."

J.T. slept at the hotel that night. All he had for supper was birthday cake with blue icing. Then he said he was going to take a long shower and get into bed, and that was when my mother invited him to have supper with us. She did it in front of everybody: Braulia, Papá, my classmates, and some of the mothers who had come with them. He thanked her but said he'd been flying all day and suspected he'd be asleep as soon as his head hit the pillow. I looked at Mamá: I thought I'd never forgive her. I looked at Papá: I hated him for forgiving everything.

The next day was Sunday, and the Captain sent Braulia to wake me. It was before seven, but I didn't care about getting up early. I dressed quickly, gulped down some crackers, and in the doorway I ran into my father, who was already awake and had offered to drive us in the truck to the airstrip at Mosquito. The Captain invited him to come with us, fifteen or twenty minutes at the most to fly over the submarines and see them from a height. Papá didn't answer right away, but then he accepted and I felt sorry for him. While I was feeling sorry I had a hateful thought: what would my life have been like if instead of being my father's son I had been the Captain's? While the plane taxied before takeoff, I looked at J.T.'s face: it wasn't the face of a father. I was asking myself questions I'd never asked before: would my mother have preferred me to be this man's son? And, if I were, would she have loved me more because instead of looking like Frank Yasín I looked like John Timothy Bunker, with his reddish hair and freckled hands, their nails black with motor oil, voracious, outlaw hands capable of grasping everything between heaven and earth that came their way?

We saw the submarines, not in the place where J.T. had seen them the previous afternoon but farther to the south. We kept going because it was forbidden to circle over them, and near the coast of St. Thomas we spotted a pack of dolphins. The Captain descended so we could watch them leap over the *pañuelitos* that he called "whitecaps"—the foam that formed on the crest of the waves. Then we turned around and again passed over the gigantic shadows roaming the bottom. I asked how many men could fit in a submarine, if there were any more modern than the ones we were looking at, and if there was any difference between submerging in warm seas, like the ones around the islands, and being under the colder waters full of pieces of ice that we saw in the movies. Between them Papá and J.T. answered as many questions as they could, or gave as many answers as they could think up; neither one knew very much about submarines. The Captain turned on the radio, we listened to music, a nice breeze was blowing that morning, and the Cessna flew without sudden movements. For a few minutes I thought we were returning to the past, becoming the people we'd been before last Christmas: my papá and J.T. friends for many years, and I the son without confusion, the boy with no wounds or any suspicions at all.

As we were landing in Mosquito, the Captain said something rapidly that I couldn't understand. My father answered in English, muttering another hurried phrase. I looked up in curiosity, raising my nose like a hare that smells danger. All I wanted was to capture some meaning in the air, but they both continued speaking in an English filled with words that were incomplete or incomprehensible. I realized they were doing it intentionally in order to keep something from me. When the plane landed they were somber, and I felt a sudden alarm inside, the presence of a dark menace moving silently beneath our feet like the silhouette of the submarines. As soon as we were back in Martineau, the Captain took off in his old Willys for Isabel Segunda, where he said he had to pick up something. I looked through the window at the wake of smoke and dust left behind by the Jeep. My father sat down to make a list of supplies needed in the hotel, and I went to find Mamá to tell her about the submarines but didn't see her anywhere in the house. I looked for her in her room and in the kitchen; generally she didn't sit down to sew on Sundays. My hands felt cold as ice. For months they'd turned to ice each time she was out of sight. I ran to ask Braulia if she knew where she was.

"She went to Mass," she said simply.

"She never goes to Mass," I protested.

"Well she goes now, what do you think about that?"

Braulia was cleaning chickens. I used to like watching her when she did that: the gardener would give her the plucked bird, and she'd cut it up, first the neck and then the feet, and finally she'd slit it open with the knife and put her hand all the way into the opening. You could hear a faint sound of escaping gases, and then she'd pull out her hand and show it to me, overflowing with intestines.

"Now all of us ought to pray," Braulia declared in a solemn tone. "Things are going to happen, I can see it in these guts."

She lifted them in her hand and held them in front of her eyes, while drops of blood fell on the table. All of that made me sick, and deep down it also scared me. I wanted to ask her who had taken my mother to church since we'd been using the truck. But I sensed that Braulia was not going to answer that or any other question. In her way, she was suffering too, feeling the absence of Gertrudis, who had left the hotel a month earlier and returned to her ranch, that kingdom we didn't know; she may have written to Braulia from there, or maybe not. I didn't know about that when I was twelve. I think now she did, she did write to her, and it may have been in one of those letters that she gave her ultimatum: either Braulia left her job at the hotel and moved in with her or they wouldn't see each other again. In December, a few weeks after our world collapsed around us, Braulia said goodbye to my father, packed her bags, and went off to live with Gertrudis.

"You ought to be in church too," she grumbled, rinsing her hands. "Where'd you go with the Captain?"

I didn't want to answer. I turned to leave the kitchen, and as I walked through the door I was stung by her voice: "Don't tell me, Andrés, you don't have to. Your Captain always tells me everything."

I stopped and shouted an insult at her. I shouted it in English, my face twisted in anger: "Bitch!" She half-closed her eyes; she was as strong as a man, and she gave me a malicious smile. "You can call me whatever you want. The Captain and I will talk soon enough."

Hatred stung in my stomach and in my own guts, where no-body would be seeing any future.

"Bitch, bitch, bitch!"

*I suspected they were watching your father. Maybe it was true, maybe not. But I warned him. And I remember the exact words I said: "You're in their sights, Frank." We were talking in the plane on the way back from a flight to St. Croix. We spoke in English, using unusual words so you wouldn't know what was going on. You sat between us; I can't remember now why the hell you were with us. I remember only what I told your father: that I'd seen two men prowling around the hotel. Maybe it was the presence of the barber or of Roberto, who'd just gotten out of jail, that attracted the police. Your father also suspected he was being watched; I knew because of how he reacted that day, a little frightened, hostile in a way. To make matters worse, there was a lot of tension between your mother and him. It was in the air, and everybody was aware of it; maybe not you because you were a child. But Estela was getting ready to run off and even tried to excuse herself to me. In a very hard, cutting way, but she did it. She planned to abandon her home and husband, not abandon you completely but leave you in Martineau temporarily; she knew you'd be safe there and it was all you knew. She wanted to leave before the uprising, but as it turned out the uprising had to be moved up; things got complicated and she had to resign herself to the delay. All she was waiting for was a signal from Roberto; it was up to him to decide the date. Though they didn't even have a place to live. He was staying with friends, a week here and a week there. And I'm sure some woman must have offered him shelter because he was good-looking; the maids at the hotel said he was fantastic.*

*According to what I could find out, he was married, and his wife, or maybe somebody else, maybe a lover of his in Isabel Segunda, came to Martineau to see your mother. Roberto came from there, from the Luján district, and was much younger than we were; he died when he was twenty-seven or twenty-eight years old, a boy no matter how you look at it. That woman, whoever she was, intercepted a letter from your mother, a few lines in which she surely talked about their leaving. According to Braulia, the woman came to the hotel and threatened your mother with a scandal and said she'd tell her husband everything. But Estela threw her out, not without first assuring her it was too late because she herself was taking care of telling her husband everything. In any case, Roberto didn't have a steady job either: the nationalists were screwed in a lot of ways, but he more than any of them because he'd been in prison. In that situation, it was difficult for him to make a new life with any woman. If in fact he really intended to make a new life, because now I'm not so sure. Your mother, as high-minded and cerebral as she seemed, was also something of a daydreamer. Buried in that hotel on the beach day after day, living the double routine of the house and the guests, maybe she clung to the only idyll in which there wasn't the slightest possibility of salvation.*

*I know what you're thinking: that these are the last spiteful tricks of a miserable old man. I don't deny it: there must be a lot of spite left in me. But just look back for a moment, stop and think what kind of life that was for Estela, knowing she was pretty and feeling her youth. Do you know what I read once in one of those travel magazines? The employees and owners of small hotels, people who spend a lot of time in those places, get sick with boredom. Instead of giving them a feeling of change, the coming and going of guests drowns them in monotony. There was a time when I knew I was breaking that monotony. I'd show up in my plane, with my stories and my bouts of drinking, and chase away your mother's boredom. But the years, and the way I became fond of being with her—the way I fell in love with her, in fact—made me as monotonous as your father. Or as predictable as you. There's nothing more predictable for a mother than her own child. Though that doesn't mean*

*Estela didn't love you; it means not even your presence was enough to keep her. She once said she'd have liked to be an actress. Roberto had something of the actor in him; I think he had worked in the theater, or on radio soap operas. He was a personage, and the little he said he said in his perfect voice. So perfect that he opened his mouth and the rest of us disappeared.*

*On the same day that I warned your father about the men prowling around the hotel, I happened to run into Estela in Isabel Segunda. Though "happened to run into" may not be the exact phrase: the truth is I went there to find her. I went to town saying I had to pick up some packages, but I was determined to surprise her. Braulia told me your mother had gone to Mass, and when she said that, we stood there looking at each other. She saw it in my eyes right away, she guessed what was going through my mind, but she didn't dare ask me to stand back and not interfere in Estela's life. Her real concern wasn't your mother; all her loyalties were with Frank, and it was Frank she was trying to protect. She saw me gasp for air, and she saw me as she'd never seen me before: troubled and deeply wounded.*

*I took the Jeep and drove to town like a madman. I went straight to the house of that woman who was Estela's friend, more Roberto's friend than hers. Her name was Antonia, and she didn't know me at all. She opened the door, and I pushed her aside without saying a word. She tried to protest, but time was pressing and she chose to protect a little boy who was playing in the living room, pushing a car around the floor. I don't know if he was her son; she looked a little old to be the mother of a two- or three-year-old. She picked him up and slipped out to the street. I went to the back of the house. Along the way I opened a door; it was a perfectly tidy bedroom with no one in it. I opened another door to what was the bedroom of a child, perhaps the same one I'd seen, and of another, older boy: there were two beds and different kinds of toys, and I was extraordinarily disturbed by the sight of a tricycle hanging on the wall.*

*At the end of the hall I could see the light that I associated with the brightness of a courtyard, a kitchen, an open dining room filled with sunlight. I let myself be guided by smell; I could smell your mother, I knew I'd find her at any moment, and when I did, she'd be smoking a cigarette and smiling behind the imprecise wreathes of smoke. The hall came to an end, and in effect, I walked into a little garden full of hearts-ease: just as I'd imagined it, I saw the kitchen and beside it a small din-ing room. Your mother was sitting, a cup of coffee in front of her. Roberto was standing; he was the one who was smoking, and the smoke from his cigarette, as if obeying an order, floated over to Estela and clouded her face. If they were surprised to see me, they didn't show it. They both turned their heads, but I didn't see surprise or hesitation or even anger. Roberto raised the cigarette to his lips and inhaled with all the self-assurance in the world. Your mother gave me a superior look and then, in a voice still warmed by talking to the other man, said: "What are you doing here?"*

*In a sense, I should have asked myself the same question. What the hell was I doing with the two of them, in front of your mother and un-der the mistrustful eyes of that man, who'd grasped everything right away? He at least knew what he was doing. His glance told me he did; he was hoping I'd get out of there without delay.*

*"Did something happen in Martineau?"*

*I began to crumble. That question of your mother's and the arrogant way she asked it indicated only one thing: I was nobody, not even her husband, I was just an interloper, an imbecile interrupting something vi-tal, sniffing at a private scent that was fierce and unreachable. I looked first at her and then at him. But finally I concentrated on Estela's face, at her lips painted bright orange and at the determined fury I found in her eyes. I realized she was throwing me out of that place and out of her life, even out of the hotel and the entire island, if necessary.*

*"You," I roared, a roar that came out enveloped in smoke and stink. "You fucking bitch!"*

*She stopped Roberto, who had started to move toward me. She stopped him like a queen, with her snow-white hand, not looking at him because she didn't stop looking into my eyes. She moved her fingers,*

*indicating that he should remain still, and the gesture was also a sign to
me. I understood that I'd fallen to the very bottom, that my total sub-
mersion was a question of minutes.*

*"You're drunk," your mother said with a sigh. "Go back to the ho-
tel and ask Braulia to make you a cup of coffee."*

*If I hadn't been so destroyed inside, I'd have laughed. The breeze
surrounded me with a trace of perfume, and the perfume acted like a
small deception. Was there the slightest possibility of setting things
right? An invisible hope with your mother? Now I look back, back fifty
years, and I see a weakling, a big, docile man, a miserable wretch who
staggers out of that house as if he really were overwhelmed by drunkenness and not horror, the machete blow that splits his skull. I left split in
two, and for a long time I had the feeling I was walking as if I'd been
hacked to pieces. The possibility of denouncing them to the police passed
through my mind, I can't deny I thought about it. They were all done
for, cleaning their pistols and making bombs to begin their shitty revolution. If I lifted a finger, I'd be rid of Roberto. But Frank was involved,
and there are loyalties that can't be touched. You'll ask me, Andrés,
what kind of loyalty excluded his wife. And the truth is I wouldn't
know how to answer you, because Estela was always a separate matter,
removed from my devotion to your father and the brotherly relationship
that developed over the years. I remember her posing for the camera,
holding you in her arms, her back to the ocean and the warship carrying
President Roosevelt. You were a year, a year and a half old. She was
barely twenty. I saw her profile and fixed on her nose, which was very
straight and spiritual and kept things at a distance. That was my first
impression, and what I invented afterward—my constant flights between
Vieques and Isla Grande, between Vieques and St. Croix, when I could
have made more money flying the plane to the Windward Islands—was
an excuse to see her again. My need to have her nearby, or to hear her
voice (sometimes I was content simply to hear her), brought me closer to
your father. This doesn't mean he and I were involved; there are words
that are misinterpreted over time. But let's say we had a connection that
was unusual; we understood each other, and now I think that behind*

*our understanding was a satisfaction, a security, an impossible pact. When you're the age I am now, with a body eaten by cancer, you understand that what move us are these small pacts, and the path a man takes is based on this.*

*When I left your mother and her lover—you'll forgive me for calling things by their right names—I went back to the hotel and, in fact, asked Braulia to make me some coffee. She only had to look at me to know I'd found Estela in Isabel Segunda, and in addition to having found her, or perhaps because of it, I was almost in tatters. She put the cup in front of me and kept looking at me while I took elemental sips; we were alone in the kitchen, and she used an ambiguous voice that seemed ghostly to me: "This won't last."*

*Who knows what she was referring to: to Estela's relationship with her childhood friend, to your father's situation, which in a way was more awkward than mine, or to my own head turned into dust, humiliated dust.*

*"It won't last," she insisted, pouring more coffee without my asking for it. "Poor Andrés is suffering more than you."*

*She was thinking about you. People give priority to children, especially at times like those. I finished the coffee, went up to my room for my suitcase, and left the way I had come. I drove blind to the Mosquito airstrip. Later, when I took off, I squeezed my eyes shut and deliberately maintained the blindness. The Cessna didn't lose its self-control. That machine was a good beast, and years later I sold it, as a good beast, to a collector in Brownwood. I've heard it still flies and is no longer called Little Parakeet but Calamity. That should have been my name too.*

# CHAPTER NINE

IN the middle of October, I dreamed about the excursion and about the light on the water. I dreamed about my mother's sandals, which in the dream fell into the ocean, and I dreamed about the crabs trapped in cardboard boxes. The dream was the memory of a past trip, an excursion my father organized when I was eight or nine years old. The guests wanted to visit the luminescent bay, and at first Papá told them it was a difficult trip. But one afternoon, without prior notification, he suggested they take a nap because that night we'd go to Barracuda. That was the name of the bay.

Since we didn't all fit in the truck, Papá rented two vehicles. At that time the hotel guests included an American family with three children; two women, mother and daughter, who came from New Jersey; an artist from San Juan ("artist" is what Braulia called her), an old, mysterious singer who wore a broad-brimmed hat day and night and therefore always required a good amount of space.

We left late in the afternoon, and night fell as soon as we stopped at Barracuda. Braulia had prepared sandwiches and brought several thermoses of coffee, and so the guests spent the time eating and talking among themselves, or eating and playing poker. Papá had hired a fisherman to pick us up in his launch at about midnight and take us to the middle of the bay, where you had the best view of the glow in the water. The American family had a boy my age (the other two, who were twins, were still small), and I spent the time with him setting ambushes for iguanas and capturing crabs that we kept in the empty sandwich boxes. I haven't forgotten the smell of those animals, the rustle of their movements inside the boxes that still contained crumbs. And I haven't forgotten the figure of Mamá in capri pants and sandals, her blond hair twisted into a snood, holding a cup of coffee in one hand and a cigarette in the other, fascinated by the phosphorescence of the waves, which was like fire.

At eleven sharp the fisherman arrived and anchored his boat a few feet from shore, and we all had to wade through the water to get onboard. A breeze was blowing, small gusts that gave us goose bumps, but since the day had been hot, the water was warm. We held our shoes as we walked, and when we reached the launch the fisherman helped us to climb in. He simply picked up the children, holding us under the armpits. I was already on deck when it was my mother's turn. Her pants had gotten wet, and she tossed me her sandals for safekeeping; I felt a certain apprehension, a strange embarrassment when I pressed them against my chest. Then they helped her in: my father pushed from below, and from above the fisherman took both her arms. She fell beside me, weak with laughter, I handed her the sandals, and we moved to one side to make room for the guests. The fisherman, however, had stopped paying attention to the people trying to board and was concentrating on Mamá's face, as if he had just recognized her. Perhaps he only recognized her laugh. She was laughing a good deal as she dried her wet feet.

"Do you remember me?" the man asked with a smile. "I'm Joaquín, the fisherman from Media Luna. Didn't Mr. Bunker come with you today?"

He asked the question and looked around, searching for the Captain. Mamá stopped laughing, stopped breathing. She lowered her head, and I had no way to look into her eyes or see how her face tightened, no question it tightened. At that time I was still enthusiastic about J.T.'s presence, and so I gave a little jump on the deck of the launch, looked toward the shore, and searched for him in vain.

"Is the Captain coming?" I touched my mother's shoulder. "Is it true he's coming?"

She lifted her head and ordered me to be still because she was feeling seasick. She shot the fisherman a glance filled with rancor, an icy glance the man could not endure. I heard him stammer: "Excuse me," and saw him shrink, fold into himself, disappear completely. I insisted on asking my mother about the Captain, I wanted to know if he was coming or not, and she replied that he wasn't and I should be quiet. In a little while we set off for the middle of the bay, moving slowly, talking among ourselves and impatient to see the spectacle. The coast was a fair distance away when the fisherman threw some buckets overboard, filled them with water, and hauled them up in order to pour the contents on the deck. We all put out our hands to bathe them in the liquid light, all of us except my mother, who seemed dazed, smiling only out of obligation, her mind somewhere else. We sailed for some time, and before we returned to land the old, mysterious singer removed her picture hat and asked that one of those buckets of water be poured over her. She closed her eyes and let herself be soaked, and as a result she gleamed for a few moments, like a decrepit virgin, her gray hair covered by brilliance. Then she dried herself with the towels Braulia had brought along, and in the silence of the night she sang a simple song in German (Papá whispered to me that it was German) that made the women from New Jersey cry and in a sense upset my mother.

That was the last time we saw Barracuda, because the bay lay inside the occupied territory, and a few weeks after our excursion the Navy completely prohibited access to it. But three years later, in October 1950, I relived the trip in my dreams even though it wasn't entirely the same: instead of the American boy, the one who ambushed iguanas with me was Santa, and she was the one who put into my hands a motionless, fragrant crab as hard as a rock. I told my father about it (the whole dream except the part about Santa) and asked him if we could go back someday. He replied that we'd be sure to go back, to Barracuda and to Puerto Diablo, where I'd had my picture taken as a little boy, and to another spot I hadn't visited yet, called Playa Púrpura, with reddish sand that tinted people's skin and caused bloody mirages on the ocean bottom.

Ever since the day I called her "bitch," Braulia and I had been distant. It's true she never told my father. But it was worse than if she had, because in revenge she stopped talking to me, and besides not talking to me she became my ironic enemy, as silent as a serpent. Mamá was nervous; at times she was startled for no reason if she saw me come into her sewing room unexpectedly, or if my father called to her from the courtyard—he'd always called to her from there. When these things happened, she'd look at us in surprise, as if astonished to see us, and then she'd respond with boredom, with a dislike (there's no other term for it) that transformed her into something different, something very removed from what she had been.

Santa, the dead Santa, came back in a powerful way. In addition to dreaming about her being on the excursion to Barracuda, I kept dreaming about her in her house in Isabel Segunda, and in Vidal's barbershop, where she'd never been, and finally I dreamed about her inside a glass case, not eating or drinking, sitting like Urbano, the Hunger Artist. In the months since her death, I hadn't wanted to go back to Matilde's house to drop off or pick up laundry. Papá had asked me to go with him, but I always gave an excuse, and in the end he realized that in my mind the road there had been closed. Though at times I was tempted by the idea of behaving as if nothing had happened: going back to her house, walking around the courtyard, spying on her from the washtubs, cautiously going up to the shed where they kept the bleach, and once I was inside, breathing in her smell. I wondered if the strength of my mind would be enough to wipe out the tragedy and make her come back.

You spend your life clinging to the same fantasy: waking the dead, bringing them out of their indifference, teaching them to walk again and to see the world. I had the same thought months after my mother's death. I had been discharged from the hospital and could go back to Vieques and my house but not back to school. I spent the days not doing anything, sitting on the beach or in the hotel—except on weekends, when some friends from Isabel Segunda would come to see me—and at the moments of greatest sadness, I thought that if I closed my eyes, squeezed my lids tight, and asked for it as hard as I could, Mamá would appear in a simple place—her sewing room, for example—a little bewildered but essentially the same, and then I'd tell her that Braulia wasn't with us anymore and another woman was in her place, that Elodio Brito was still cooking and Gerónimo was pruning plants, but Papá was talking about selling the hotel, and if he couldn't sell it right away he said he'd close it for a while.

At the time I dreamed about Barracuda, a good number of guests passed through Martineau. Men and women who'd spend a night at the hotel and leave the next day. Toward the end of October, two couples arrived; they seemed like two married couples who were very good friends, a little older than my parents. After they registered and dropped their bags in their rooms, they put on their bathing suits and ran to the beach, to the shore that was full of jellyfish. My father, who almost never went into the ocean, put on striped shorts and went out after them. At lunchtime Roberto showed up. He came to the house and asked that Estela be told; he spoke to Braulia, who happened to be there and who said to me drily: "Go up and tell your mother."

I went to find her and didn't have to tell her anything, because as soon as she saw my face, she guessed that someone had arrived. She passed me in a flash, ran down the stairs, and from the second floor I saw that she held her hand out to Roberto, a hand that I imagined was cold. Her voice was husky, she tossed back her hair, her blond mane that had become disheveled in her rush, and said that Frank was already on the beach with their friends from San Juan, and they undoubtedly were waiting for him. Roberto replied that he had to change his clothes, and Mamá said of course, he could use the bathroom. While he was changing, she and I sat on the sofa, staring at the door as if we were waiting for a great show to begin. Braulia, in the meantime, went into the kitchen and returned with a cup of coffee. She placed it on the end table and waited with us, not opening her mouth.

Roberto came back in shorts. He had unbuttoned his shirt, and underneath he was wearing a white undershirt. Instead of his lace-up shoes, he wore slippers for walking in the sand. Braulia pointed to the coffee. "Drink it before it gets cold."

She spoke to him with authority, as if she were addressing a child or a servant. My mother also noticed her tone and turned toward Braulia, and a slow look passed between them that was too charged, or too difficult. Roberto finished the coffee and handed her the cup. "Very good," he murmured. "As always."

After he'd gone out to the beach, Mamá asked me to go up with her to the sewing room. When we got there, she closed the door, dropped into her chair, and said: "Don't even think about going to the beach now."

I thought she'd read my mind, because that was precisely what I was planning to do: go to the beach, join my father, and since we couldn't swim because of the jellyfish, collect crabs or clams for Elodio Brito to cook with rice.

"Your father has to talk with those guests. He asked me to tell you not to go."

I looked at her suspiciously; I was beginning to distrust her words.

"Don't you dare show up there," she added, and she also seemed to guess my plans to defy her: "You heard me, Andrés Yasín, now go and study."

I went downstairs, walked around the house a few times, and went into the bathroom where Roberto had changed. I pulled down my zipper and began to urinate for pleasure, not really feeling I had to. When I looked up, I saw a dark leather bag on one of the highest shelves, not very well hidden behind a couple of towels. I climbed up on the toilet and took it down without thinking very much about what I was doing. I put it on the floor carefully, because I knew it was Roberto's bag. In it were his shoes and trousers, an unopened pack of cigarettes, some keys, a folded newspaper, and at the bottom, under everything else, I found a pistol. I took it out slowly and looked at it. I pointed it at the mirror. I pointed it at the ceiling. I pointed it at my heart. Then I went to the window and pointed it at the courtyard. I thought it was a shame Braulia wasn't out there because I'd have pointed it at her, too. I put the weapon back and walked out of the bathroom drenched in perspiration. It was a summery October, with air as thick as marmalade. Air that was slightly dead and hard to breathe.

"YOU'RE talking to a dead man," the Captain blustered. "Do you think a dead man would beat around the bush?"

He looked withered, but his color was better. They'd put him to sleep and given him oxygen. They'd injected I don't know how much fluid into his veins to wash out the liquor. None of the doctors dared prescribe any other medicine that could cause complications. They only tried to revive him enough so he could go back to Maine, and by the next day they were ready to discharge him. His bags were packed; I had taken out the change of clothes he'd wear when he left the hospital, went to the airport, and took the plane to New York. His son would meet him in New York and accompany him to Maine.

"I wasn't your father's best friend. I can't say that, but I almost was. There was a piece of his life he never wanted to talk about with me. Though I did know about the uprising; I could see and smell everything, and for a long time I asked myself why he went on with that adventure. I knew Frank was a nationalist, I always knew he had those ideas, because old Apolonia had instilled them in him. But it's one thing to have a conviction and it's a very different thing to become completely involved in an absurdity. The curious thing is that Estela supported him from the very beginning. Nobody had instilled anything in her (her father was a tyrant, a lying, dirty old man), but your mother married very young, she was almost a child, and because they went to live with Apolonia, your grandmother had to have influenced her. In time, Estela met the nationalists in the group, and among them was Roberto, who happened to be a childhood friend of hers, both of them godchildren of the same woman, a circumstance that must have brought them together, I suppose. Don't you think those kinds of things bring people together?"

J.T. dared to smile and waited for my reply. I looked at him with these slanted eyes and their drooping lids, the eyes of a defeated old Lebanese. I thought about everything I could have done at that moment: cover his face with a pillow, for example, or punch him in the chest. I also thought about the consequences: I was very old to be attacking another damn old man. It would have been ridiculous: the nurses would come to separate us, and when they found me so obstinate, so out of control, they'd ask for help from the men who distribute the food, who tend to be brawny. Or the women who do the cleaning, they're brawny too, and accustomed to the cruel blows in hospitals.

"You're not saying anything, Andrés. I know very well what you're thinking. You're thinking something not even your father dared to think: you see in me the great informer, the treacherous gringo who had more than one reason to bring down the uprising. But remember: you're talking to a dead man, and this corpse can swear to you his mouth never uttered a single word that could have ruined their party. On the contrary, it had been ruined from the start, which is why I gave your father advice. From the outside, from my vantage point, I could see better than anybody how it was curdling, and I thought the whole thing could turn into a trap. I warned him very calmly. We stayed up one night toward the end of October. I was leaving for St. Croix the next day and didn't intend to return for two or three weeks. Your father also had a trip planned to Isla Grande, the port of Fajardo, I think, where the nationalists were going to hold a meeting. He wasn't very fond of attending meetings, but rumors were flying that there would be an attempt on the life of their leader, Albizu, and everyone had been asked to be present to defend him if anything happened. Estela would gladly have gone with him, but they didn't want to leave you alone; somebody had to take you to school the next morning and somebody would have to care for you if things became complicated. Frank confided that he planned to take the Luger he'd put away (I knew that pistol, I'd helped him get it), but in the end I don't know if he took it with him."

J.T. stopped speaking when he saw the nurse come in. She took his temperature and pulse and checked the IV line. She was fat and had a stern face that was very black and very broad. Before she left us alone, she whispered in a blues singer's voice: "You're leaving tomorrow, Grandpa." The old man followed her with his eyes; she was so big she stirred the air when she walked.

"I don't know if Frank picked up the Luger," the Captain continued. "I said we were up the whole night, but we didn't talk the whole time. We were smoking and drinking too, especially smoking, thinking our own thoughts. When you're in your thirties, you can be up the whole night and drink as much as you like and not even notice it the next day. That's why we were there, on one of the hotel balconies, in no hurry to go to bed. After a brief period of silence, your father suddenly said: 'I don't know what to do about Estela.' I went on smoking and looking straight ahead, in the direction of the beach that couldn't be seen because it was completely dark, but it could be heard: we breathed in the salt air and listened to the waves, the mountainous sound of high tide. 'I don't know what to do,' he repeated. 'I'm waiting for all this to be over before I decide.' *All this to be over* meant the uprising, the moment of confronting the government and the police, which he knew was very close. Perhaps there, that night, alone with me, he began to cling to the same secret hope I could have clung to, not expressing it in words, of course, but encouraged by my complicity, by the support I was giving him. Roberto in jail or dead (better dead than anything else) was no longer a threat to him or, of course, to me. It was impossible for us to say it—nobody wants to feel contemptible, or even to seem contemptible—but I assure you we were thinking it. In our situation it was inevitable. How could Frank not think about it when he saw his home collapsing, his wife leaving him, his world coming to an end? And how could I not think about it? I didn't have anything like a home, but it was as if I did have one, because coming to Martineau, sitting at the table, talking to your father, kidding around with Braulia was the closest thing I'd ever had to a home, to a family complete with child. I want you to know that back then I was fond of you. In my own way I was crazy about you. And I know that secretly you admired me, had a good time with me, waited for me so you could climb into Eugene the Jeep: you had the best time with that old jalopy. Until you became jealous, began to feel like a man and challenged me and discovered some phantoms between your mother and me. They were phantoms, don't have any doubt about that. No matter how much I might have wanted you to be right or wished that your reasons for hating me had been based on a real romance. But by then, and for a few years before that, I'd been less than nothing in Estela's life. I'd never been very much, if truth be told, and over time I became less and less and less. I'm at the doors of the next world, where maybe I'll see her. Vanity does me no good, so what do you want me to say to you? Your mother showed me nothing but repugnance. There was no reason for it: I wasn't a dirty man, or sick, and I didn't have an unpleasant face. On the contrary, you have no idea how much I spruced up to go to see her. Sometimes I look at photographs from that time and see myself dressed in my work clothes, my cap, my aviator glasses. I wonder if I deserved that disgust, that reluctance to have me even touch her hand. I don't know how she was with your father, I don't know if he began to feel that rejection too. The night we stayed up, I would have liked to read his mind, make him bring up the pain. But he didn't want to commit himself, he said only the most basic things, what you could see coming, what even Braulia, even the guests could smell: sooner or later, Estela would run off with that man, and let me tell you, by then not even you could have stopped her. Roberto was everything to her, just like on those radio soap operas, and she almost didn't bother to hide it. So imagine how much I hated him, how much I wanted him wiped off the face of the earth, wanted him obliterated. I saw my wish come true in spades: I was longing for him to be shot, right? Well, in the end he was riddled with eighty-four bullets. How do you think I reacted when your father told me? I wanted to throw my arms around him, I could barely contain my joy. Frank was terrified because he thought they were coming to arrest him, and he looked despondent too; he felt sorry for that man and sorry to see Estela paralyzed, witless, as if the bullets had hit her as well. They did hit her, Andrés, they left her dead. And Frank, for a few days, was the deadest of all. Incapable of knowing what to feel, what to think, what hole he should hide in. I offered to take him to Martinique or the Grenadines, where I had friends who could take him in, people who wouldn't ask questions. I canceled all my flights and went back to Vieques the last day of October. I took the Jeep and raced into Martineau. Your mother wasn't seeing anyone. Your father had just arrived from San Juan; he'd escaped by the skin of his teeth, and I found him devastated; all he talked about was blood, for him everything was blood. Braulia walked around, inscrutable but efficient, looking for sedatives to give to your mother, brewing tea, taking care of you as well. She was the only one who took care of you then. She sent you to school with Gerónimo and tried to maintain calm and a semblance of normality in that house, which in the end was impossible.

"On the last day of October, around noon, your father lay down to sleep. He hadn't closed his eyes in more than forty-eight hours, and he'd lost his composure, his ability to think coldly and decide what to do. He went into one of the rooms in the hotel because it was impossible to rest near your mother: she'd have fits of weeping, she'd scratch at her arms, or sometimes she'd become enervated, and that was worse because her trembling shook the bed. When your father left to get some sleep, I went to see her. I sat beside her, stroked her head, and said as sweetly as I could: 'Estela, listen to me.' She was hoarse, her eyes were swollen, her lips were cracked because she'd bitten them so much. She was still the best woman I'd ever seen in my life, the most complete, and the strongest, because even in her collapse she kept her strength. Not her serenity, which is something else. I mean strength, the will to end it all, to break with everyone and with herself. What I saw frightened me, and what I heard, what came out of her mouth, was even more terrifying: 'What are you doing here, you damn gringo?' But in spite of that I kept repeating: 'Listen to me, please, you have to listen to me.' She burst into howls of weeping; you hadn't come home from school yet, and I was happy for you. I was happy for your father too, because he'd fallen asleep and been spared the sight of this. I didn't know how much bitterness, how much disillusionment I was capable of tolerating, but I tolerated everything. I listened to her whispering his name: she was calling for the dead man, she didn't call for you, or me, or your father, but for Roberto. I saw her get up, stagger to the bureau, and take out the packet of letters and photographs: 'Take this. Throw it into the ocean, far out into the ocean.' I wanted to put my arms around her, take her right there in that unmade bed filled with the remains of spilled tea, camomile and especially linden flower. That bed damp with sweat and tears and, I had the impression, with urine too. Your mother looked awful, her hair was wet and her face was red, and she wiped away snot with the back of her hand. But to me she was still dazzling. Then she dozed off; she hadn't been able to sleep for hours either. I saw that she was overcome by fatigue (more than sleep, it was like a stupor), and I tiptoed out. Braulia was in the living room; she looked at me wearily and asked if I wanted to drink one of her concoctions. I said I needed rum, a whole bottle, and she, without saying a word, went out one door as you came in the other. You tossed your book bag onto a table and looked at me suspiciously; there was a strange odor in the air, and an even stranger, more urgent silence, like a faint whistle. You asked for your father. I said he'd been very tired when he came home from San Juan and was sleeping in the hotel. Then you asked for Estela. I told you that she wasn't feeling well and that Braulia was looking after her. You'd already seen her despair, because the news of Roberto's death had come the day before, a little after noon, and at first she hadn't believed it, but after a few hours, when it was certain it was true, she didn't bother to hide anything, she wasn't careful even though you were there. She showed that she didn't care about anything anymore, not even your father, who was still in San Juan.

"Braulia came back with the bottle and put it in front of me: 'Drink it all up, Captain,' she said in a quiet voice, and then, with a very disagreeable face, she told you to wash up and have a snack. It was almost three o'clock, and I realized I was in the way. I poured a drink, gulped it down, and poured another. You ignored Braulia's orders and stood right in front of me to watch me drink, wearing an expression I thought was perverse. At that moment Gerónimo came in—I think it was Gerónimo, though it might have been Elodio Brito, the cook. Whoever it was, he was agitated and gasping for air. 'Turn on the radio,' I remember him shouting. 'They're killing the barber.' I looked around for a radio, but you were ahead of me; you ran to the table and turned it on at full volume. We listened to the explosions, the whirlwind of a voice obsessively repeating the names of two streets, Colton at the corner of Barbosa, and the name of the barbershop: Salón Boricua. Inside, according to the man narrating the siege, the nationalists were hiding; at first they believed there were several of them, but in the end they learned there was only one person barricaded in there: the barber Vidal. Out of nowhere your father appeared, with his shirt open and the horrified expression of someone who has gone down to hell and hasn't climbed all the way out. And out of nowhere, not making any noise, your mother appeared too. I didn't have to look behind me toward the stairs to know she was sitting on the bottom steps, with her madwoman's hair and her swollen lips, trying to hear the news reporting on the number of rifles and carbines, all those weapons vomiting fire into the barbershop. I'd never heard a silence like it, one more compact, more incredibly desolate. The only thing you could hear was the voice on the radio betting that the barber was still alive, that he'd stay inside until he died. I poured your father a drink, and I poured another drink to take to Estela. But she stopped me before I reached her; with a single look she let me know she didn't need any help. On the radio you could still hear the firing outside the barbershop and the heavy breathing of the man who was speaking: he gasped at times, crouching behind barrels to avoid the bullets. I got sick of all of it and left the house. I went up to my room in the hotel and looked out the window at the ocean. It was the only thing that hadn't changed. The only thing in a world where everything, inevitably, had changed."

HERE my life breaks in two: sometime between the last day of October and the first day of November. When everything happened, Papá tried to give some coherence to the tragedy; he wrote a letter that was also a will, to be given to me if anything happened to him. But nothing did happen to him, and for years he held on to it. He waited until I'd grown and graduated, until I'd come home from Vietnam and was about to marry Gladys. The night before my wedding, the two of us went out for supper. Not long after we sat down, he handed me a sealed envelope and said it was a poor gift, but he hadn't been able to destroy it without my reading it. He added that there were issues we'd never talked about, and perhaps the letter would clarify some doubts for me. It wasn't very long, and it was dated November 6, 1950, which meant he wrote it while I was convalescing in the hospital, dehydrated and half-crazed. I said I wanted to read it right away. We both were having the same drink. Scotch and soda. My father murmured: "Whatever you like, Andrés."

He lit a cigarette and sat looking at me while I opened the envelope and took out the sheets of very thin paper, yellowed by the years. He began the letter by telling me the reasons for the uprising: to proclaim the Republic and prevent approval of the constitution that would serve as the basis for consummating the farce—he underlined that word: *farce*—the semblance of self-government without power or sovereignty. But it all fell apart. The uprising had to be moved ahead because the authorities were watching them day and night, closing in on them, and they could barely manage to shake off the police long enough to have a meeting. On October 27, very close to the barber's house, the police stopped a car carrying a group of nationalists; all their weapons were confiscated, and bombs were found in the trunk. This was Friday. For the rest of that day and for the entire weekend they did not stop their searches. My father insisted there were only two alternatives: either they began the revolution right then, or they'd rot in prison without even making an attempt. They received orders to begin the revolt on Monday, October 30. And so on Sunday my father left for San Juan. He traveled in the passenger launch, carrying only a small valise. He said goodbye to me, though I may not have realized the intensity of that farewell. In a different but equally intense way, he said goodbye to my mother. He spent the night in a small hotel in Santurce, whose owner he knew because he'd been a friend of Apolonia's since the days when my grandmother had her guesthouse in Isabel Segunda. Papá hardly slept. He smoked one cigarette after another, and at three in the morning he took a long shower to clear his head. Then he went out to the balcony, and for a while he looked at the deserted streets, gleaming with the brilliance left by successive downpours. From the balcony he saw the blue Dodge in which his friends had said they'd pick him up. It was ten minutes past four in the morning. From the hotel they drove south of the city, to the Buen Consejo district. In the courtyard of Raimundo Díaz's house—he was a commander of the Liberating Army—they improvised a barracks. They changed their clothes, loaded their weapons, drank coffee, and heard their final orders. Only then, as he was smoking in the courtyard, was my father informed that he wouldn't be in the group of men going to attack the governor's house, the Fortaleza. At the last minute they decided to replace him with the barber Vidal, who was waiting for them at the barbershop. The reason they gave for excluding him was very simple: they thought he could be more useful in the support plan that would follow the uprising, since he wasn't being watched and nobody knew him in San Juan. Though the Captain kept insisting that my father was in their sights, he stated that it was nothing, that the men J.T. had seen prowling around the hotel were probably from his own party, nationalists taking care of security.

At midmorning, Papá left Buen Consejo and went back to the hotel in Santurce. Nobody stopped him, and he didn't notice anyone following him. Depending on what happened, he had instructions either to coordinate new attacks or to return home quickly. From that moment on he became part of a rearguard whose duty was to wait for the outcome of the initial actions. At midday he had lunch at a restaurant near the hotel. And at one o'clock he went up to his room, but not for very long, because he was desperate to hear the news. He went down to the lobby and saw the employees crowded around the radio: the men who had attacked the Fortaleza were all dead, and elsewhere on the island dozens of insurrectionists had fallen. He went back to his room and hardly left it again until the next day. No one came to give him orders, and no one attempted to communicate with him to receive any.

At five in the morning he left his lair, paid the bill, and returned to Vieques on the same passenger launch he'd taken when he left. During the crossing, he didn't stop looking at the ocean and thinking about his dead friends: Roberto, yes, but also Vidal. The bullets that cut short the barber's life had really been intended for him. When he reached Martineau, he ran into J.T., who'd landed a few minutes earlier in Mosquito but had heard the news and was expecting the worst. As for my mother, she was devastated. All she did was cry and tear at her arms, hysterical. Papá went to sleep in one of the rooms in the hotel; he was exhausted and admitted he couldn't think. But after two or three hours he felt someone shaking him awake. "They're going to kill the barber," Braulia told him in a cavernous tone that seemed to rise up from death itself. "The barber's dead," my father stammered. "Not yet," she insisted. "They've been shooting at the barbershop for a while now."

From that point on, the letter became frantic and obscure, and the obscurity was reflected in the writing. I began to have trouble deciphering certain words, and Papá asked me to stop reading for a moment.

"It may seem hard to you," my father acknowledged. "But if you read it calmly, in a few days you'll see everything differently."

"On my honeymoon," I answered sarcastically.

"Yes," Papá agreed. "Then you'll be safe, happy with your wife. And the calamity I'm telling you about will fade into the background."

I didn't pay attention to him right away; at all costs I wanted to read a few more paragraphs. There was bitterness and frustration, and it was clear Papá knew the identity of the person who had betrayed them. I thought about asking him straight out if he suspected the Captain, but I didn't think it very likely he would admit something like that. Papá was nervous, you could see it in his small facial contractions. He even felt the need to explain that the man sitting in front of me was not exactly the same one who had written the letter.

"I should have stayed with your mother," he lamented. "But I made the mistake of shutting myself away and falling into a daze. I didn't help her, or you either. I didn't even realize you'd gotten sick. Braulia had to tell me."

I shook my head. I hadn't realized I was sick either. It was disgust that I sank into and that separated me from the world. And the Captain was to blame. It was the moment to tell my father everything, as we sat face-to-face, talking to each other with affection, with an intimacy we hadn't felt since the days of our misfortune.

"Maybe that's why you've always had such a negative reaction to nationalism," he murmured, pulling out a thorn that was too old, yellowing and fragile like the letter I was holding.

"It isn't a reaction," I said, trying to smile. "You just can't understand how Apolonia's grandson could choose a different path and believe in other things."

"I understand," Papá countered. "That's why it hurts me. When you became old enough to decide, we were in limbo and no longer an option. The fault wasn't entirely ours. They chewed us up and spat us out, and then everybody rode over us until we were mixed with the dust, completely invisible. It isn't that they've forgotten us, Andrés, there'd be a solution for that. It's something worse: we stopped being real, we weren't what we had been even during the year when we were in so much danger. Your grandmother must have turned over in her grave. You and I left Martineau, and you saw me doing what I'm still doing: buying and selling houses for other people. For the peaceable citizens of the state of Georgia. You don't know how much I like living there."

We finished eating, and he recalled that as he was writing the letter, and during that whole month of November, he had lived in a state of continual alarm, expecting to be arrested at any moment. As a precaution, he cut off all communication with the other nationalists, and it wasn't until many months had passed that he felt capable of sending—and receiving—signs of life. By then, the new constitution was already in effect; most people favored the creation of a commonwealth with its own government, and the hope of the Republic that he and his friends had wanted to proclaim came to nothing. Less than nothing.

"So many dead," Papá concluded. "And tell me, Andrés: who in this life remembers them?"

# CHAPTER TEN

THE barber held out for more than three hours. The same ones we spent glued to the radio, hanging on the words of the reporter narrating the siege, a man who identified himself every few minutes, whispering his name into the microphone as if he were revealing a secret. J.T. left the hotel and came back half an hour later with a bottle of whiskey that he must have brought from St. Croix. From time to time he gave us a furtive glance; he looked at Braulia, a woman of stone, but she had hidden her face in her hands; and he looked at my father, who spent all that time not moving, his eyes filled with tears, staring at the floor.

I felt his glance on me too, but I pretended I hadn't, and avoided it. I didn't want to face the Captain until I could understand what was going on. And for the moment, I understood very little. That my mother, for instance, had become a complete ghost, removed from me and removed from my father, removed from the house where we lived and from the time that was passing. I also realized that a revolt had broken out, and that was why they were killing the barber, but I didn't know the exact reasons. Fifteen policemen and twenty-five national guards were at the corner of Colton and Barbosa. The bursts of gunfire were puncturing the walls of the Salón Boricua, and my mind moved back and forth between the scene described on the radio—the barbershop surrounded, clouds of smoke rising to the rooftops—and the other scene behind me: Mamá sitting at the bottom of the stairs, so rigid and absurd, already withdrawn from almost everything, trying to fathom the final horror before abandoning herself completely to that same horror.

At about five in the afternoon, the police stopped firing. The man narrating from the Barrio Obrero explained that no shots could be heard from the interior. My father looked up for the first time and exchanged glances with the Captain. Then he turned to me and said, "Andrés, go play on the beach for a while."

I said no. I did this by moving my head from side to side, filled with fury, my lips pressed tightly together; I had the feeling that if I stayed, I'd be accepting the rules of a game I didn't know and perhaps no one could explain to me. The voice on the radio became more tense, much more somber, when it announced that the police were advancing on the barbershop, moving the final obstacles aside with thrusts of their bayonets. Then we heard shouts of "This way, this way," and "We have him now," and for some minutes, the few it took him to reach the interior of the Salón Boricua, the reporter stammered phrases about broken glass and the smell of gunpowder. Then he caught sight of the barber, or what was left of him, a motionless body bathed in blood, half-hidden beneath a small mattress.

"He's still breathing," said the man on the radio. "I hear him moaning."

Transmission was abruptly cut off. Papá stood up, walked around, and dropped into the chair again. It seemed to me he'd lost his balance; his face was contorted, and his arms were like rags. "Worse for him if he's alive," he murmured.

Instinctively I looked toward the stairs. My mother was still there, but I suspected she couldn't see or hear what was going on. I felt adrift between an absent mother and a directionless father, who was about to fuse with the chair or disappear in it. The only thing to hold on to was J.T.; he'd survived and could help me. I looked at him, urging him to do something. He held

a glass filled with whiskey and took one thoughtful swallow after another, his eyes half-closed. Braulia disappeared as soon as
she heard that the police were making their way into the barbershop. I don't know if she disappeared because it made her
sick to listen to the outcome or if she did it to take her revenge.
Revenge on my mother, who was betraying Papá. And revenge
on me, who had called her a bitch. Now, however, we needed
her. I needed her there with one of her infusions, taking my
mother by the arm and obliging her to return to her room. And
I needed her next to Papá, talking to him about something having to do with the hotel, making him come back to himself. I
was sorry I hadn't listened to him when he told me to go to the
beach. I had one of those stupid fantasies that the death of the
barber, his face covered with blood and bone splinters, might
not have reached me on the beach. That in the ocean filled with
jellyfish I'd have been able to conjure away this bad dream and
turn the day, the last day of October, into an afternoon as bor-
ing and clean as all the others, with Braulia grumbling and my
father going in and out, carrying packages or tools, and Mamá
in her sewing room trying to decide between two spools of
thread that seemed identical to me, or what was even simpler:
discussing the food with Elodio Brito, the taciturn cook whose
inner life I'll never know about. I blamed myself for not going
to the beach at the right time and stopping the tragedy then and
there, like a magician, or like a child who doesn't attract death.
At that moment I was attracting death to Martineau, to Mamá,
to Braulia, to Frank Yasín, my father, who trembled in disbelief
and became dizzy and had difficulty breathing. The Captain
dropped his glass and ran to help him. "What's wrong, Frank?"
    Papá lifted his hand, telling him it was nothing. Then he
burst into tears, and his weeping froze me inside. The Captain
must have frozen too, because he went for the bottle and offered
it to Papá, who didn't notice or perhaps didn't feel like having a
drink, and J.T. was left with his arm extended, holding out the

bottle, like a statue that won't move, that will collapse if anyone dares to brush against it. This scene was more than my mother could bear, even in her lethargic state. I saw her get to her feet and go to the kitchen, and I wondered if I ought to follow her. Papá dried his tears and looked at me. He seemed small and fearful; he'd never seemed that way to me before. He called me to him with a gesture. I remembered the times my grandmother Apolonia, when she was already senile, would confuse me with her own son and ask me to approach. When I reached her side, she'd squeeze my arm to keep the wandering Lebanese from getting what he wanted.

"Nothing's going to happen to me," said Papá, the poor man not knowing what else to say to me.

He bit his upper lip, and along with his lip he bit part of his black mustache, soaked with tears or with sweat. His face was red, and his lock of hair fell onto his forehead and covered one eye. All that must have made him seem very fragile compared to me, with my scowling, tearless face, which really was a face close to exploding. I slipped into the kitchen; my mother had poured a glass of water and was staring at it. I asked where Braulia was, just for something to say. She answered in a very tranquil tone: "She must be in the hotel; somebody has to take care of the guests."

I can't remember the guests who were in Martineau at the time. In any case, only two or three rooms were occupied, including the Captain's. I know that because Papá mentioned it later; he said that fortunately, since October was the slow season, there hadn't been strangers hanging around the house in the midst of the tragedy. Mamá began to take sips of water, and I thought it was a sign she was coming back to us, to her usual life. I asked her if the barber was dead.

"I think so," she replied. "But you ought to forget about it. Tomorrow is an ordinary day, you have school."

I felt so much happiness when I heard those words that I

wanted to throw my arms around her and tell her it was the only thing that mattered to me: that tomorrow would be a day like any other, with school and boys my age, running games and teachers, coming back to Martineau for lunch in my father's truck, listening to him whistle, looking at his profile: his bushy eyebrows, his curved, camel driver's nose, and the cigarette that dangled from his lips.

Mamá smiled at me and left the kitchen after pouring another glass of water to take up to her room. When I went back to the living room, my father and the Captain had already left, and on the radio they were still talking about the attack on the barbershop, so I turned it off, and doing that made me afraid. I held my arm out in front of me as if the mere fact of approaching the radio could infect me with its madness.

That night we had supper in the hotel dining room, not in our house. Mamá didn't want to leave her room, and my father and I shared the table with J.T., who had continued to drink and by now was pretty drunk. Until that moment, until the three of us sat down at the table, I hadn't thought about what reasons my mother might have for feeling so much despair. Somehow I blamed the Captain, who had wanted to take her away with him; and I blamed my father, who had made her nervous with his sudden trip to San Juan and was away on the day of the uprising, which was precisely the day she had been listening to the news since dawn, sobbing and not eating anything. By the time Papá came back, at noon on Tuesday, it was too late to straighten things out because Mamá had crossed the frontier. It was a confused picture for someone my age, and it all happened in too short a time. But that night something told me that normality would return gradually, that the return to routine in a sense depended on me, even if I didn't know what was going on, and on Braulia, who unlike me, knew everything about everybody— there was nothing she didn't know in that house—and perhaps for this reason, because she knew so much, she was in a state of such panic that when she picked up the plates, our plates with the food almost untouched, her hands were trembling.

Papá sent me to bed so he could keep talking to the Captain. At any other time I'd have resisted, but not on that day and not in those circumstances. I had the impression that the air around us, the hotel, the very walls of my house could shatter like glass if I provoked any upset, no matter how trivial. Before I went into my room, I went to Mamá's room, slowly opened the door, and saw that none of the lights had been turned on, though some light did come in through the window. I smelled camphor, since Braulia had prepared plasters made with the leaves, which were planted everywhere—Gerónimo planted them as if our lives depended on them. Her voice came to me from the semi-darkness: "Did you want something, Andrés?"

I did want something, but I couldn't say exactly what it was. "I'm going to bed," I said.

In bed, leafing through comics, marking them with a pencil (it was an old mania of mine), I felt a peace I hadn't felt in months, perhaps not since Christmas. The next morning Braulia came to wake me; she handed me a glass of milk and said J.T. would take me to school. I asked why my father or Gerónimo wasn't driving me in the truck. She didn't answer but challenged me with a look, letting me know she still felt rancor and would continue to feel contempt for me until I surrendered. To myself I called her "bitch" again, "bitch" a thousand times. I didn't try to see Mamá or say goodbye to her. I imagined she'd stay in her room, and when I came back I'd find her recovered, back on her feet, working in the kitchen. I also supposed Papá would be in La Esperanza, buying fish, returning to the routine on which the world and the air we breathed depended.

"Are you ready?" The Captain could barely speak; his bout of drinking had left him hoarse. I got into Eugene the Jeep, the best vehicle I'd ever ridden in my life. J.T. had promised that as soon as I turned twelve he'd teach me to drive it. I was already twelve but hadn't wanted to remind him. My only wish, the only one I had with regard to him, was that he go far away from my house, from Martineau, and from my mother.

"Frank asked me to take you. I'll pick you up at midday too."

I looked at him with suspicion. He drove quickly, but he always drove like that, as if he were crossing a minefield, zigzagging to avoid the potholes in the road. Eugene the Jeep bounced along, and that was the fun in getting into an authentic Willys, one from the war: the leaps into the air that we made in response to the vehicle's bouncing, leaps that were different from any others, and when you at last got to know all the tricks, you could feel the complicity, a relationship similar to the one a rider has with his horse. The Willys was a magnificent horse.

I felt calm at school and in a sense, perhaps, relieved. As if after my fearing for months that a misfortune would occur, suddenly the misfortune had passed by without touching me. Everybody was talking about the uprising; the boys referred to the shootings on Isla Grande as if they were skirmishes in a distant war. I'd have liked to talk about the barber, but before I got out of the Jeep, J.T. had grabbed my arm and warned me that I couldn't tell anybody what I knew.

"Your father asked me to tell you this: keep your mouth shut. You could complicate things for him, and for Estela too."

I remained silent, looking at him with mistrust. No way was I going to promise him anything.

"I'll pick you up later."

But he wasn't there when I came out, and he didn't show up for the next hour. I began walking along the streets near the school, looking back from time to time in case I saw Eugene the Jeep. A restless type like the Captain would think right away that another restless type like me couldn't stay still for so long, standing in front of the school doors, looking ridiculous with his notebooks and pencil case. Another long hour went by. I got hungry and bought something at a stand on the square. In the last few minutes I had walked a good distance, so I turned and retraced my steps in case J.T. was idiot enough to stop in one place and not look for me in the surrounding area.

The idiot, however, wasn't J.T. but the gardener. At first, when I turned onto the street where the school was and saw the truck, I thought it must be my father. I began to run, filled with false hope but actually feeling that something wasn't right. I was surprised that Papá didn't start the engine and drive toward me, which was the logical thing to do. I was annoyed when I reached the truck and saw Gerónimo's livid face, which was annoyed as well, clouded by a kind of great spasm.

"Why didn't the Captain come?"

Gerónimo shrugged. "Get in," he said.

He had callused, hard hands, which always left a streak of dirt on the steering wheel.

"Where's my father?"

He moved his neck slowly. His head looked like the head of a large sea turtle, his face filled with craters, his nose broad and fleshy, his tiny eyes surrounded by fat, little lumps of fat.

"He's in the gayhow," said Gerónimo, insisting on calling the hotel "guesthouse," its name in English, which he always pronounced in his own way.

I devised another question, though I knew Gerónimo was a man of few words and too crafty ever to commit himself. I asked him if Mamá had remembered that I was in Isabel Segunda and nobody had come to pick me up. Unlike the Captain, Gerónimo drove with maddening slowness. He ignored my question and said something about hanged dogs he'd just seen. I was interested in the dogs, which distracted me for the moment. Close to Martineau he stopped the truck and pointed at a bend in the road. "There they are. I bet they were devils when they were alive."

And in fact, hanging from a bush, were two big brown dogs,

already beginning to swell, their mouths displaying final grimaces of ferocity.

"Somebody got fed up with them," Gerónimo concluded. "That happens when the devils get loose."

I shuddered. The gardener always said the little he had to say in those kinds of terms. He knew how to create an effect of anguish that kept floating in the air over people. We started driving again, and for the rest of the time, the few minutes before we arrived, he was silent. I also bit my tongue; I didn't even show surprise when I saw the car parked in front of the hotel, a Buick that was famous in Isabel Segunda because it was the only 1949 model and had vents like bull's-eyes. I knew it belonged to the doctor. I passed it and continued walking to the house. The two maids were in the doorway, along with Elodio Brito, who saw me coming and turned his back. The maids didn't move; one was whimpering without tears, staring at nothing. The other wasn't crying, but she gave me a strange look as if only then, after so many years of working for my parents, had she realized I existed.

Inside it smelled of apples. It was a smell that froze your nose. My father, Braulia, and the doctor were sitting at the table. The three of them looked at me, but Papá immediately looked away. For the first time in all those years, Braulia seemed defenseless, more dazed and frightened than when her niece Santa had died. For a few minutes no one said anything, and then Papá stood, came toward me, put his arm around my shoulders, and said we should take a walk. We passed the hotel and the Buick with its tamed eyes, crossed the street, and started down the narrow path that led to the beach. Suddenly, my father stopped.

"Listen, Andrés."

I knew what he was going to say. I looked at his desolate eyes, ravaged by so much unhappiness.

"Mamá's dead."

He kneeled so I could put my arms around him. That's what

I think because he held his arms out to me, but I didn't embrace him. I stared at the sand, all that infinite sand around the path.

"You'll find out sooner or later: your mother was feeling very sad, and she took her own life."

I've always admired the way Papá said those words, with a bleak smile that revealed to me for a moment another dimension of sleep, an unfathomable, natural mirror: the dark peace that is unleashed with death.

"She took some pills," he added, "and then she fell asleep."

Papá sat down on a piece of tree trunk and invited me to sit beside him. He lit a cigarette, took a couple of drags, and passed it to me. He'd never done anything like that before. I took it between my fingers—I knew what to do—I inhaled the smoke, and my eyes filled with tears. Then I gave it back to him. We stood, walked back to the house, passed the doctor, who was getting into his car, and passed the maids, passed Elodio Brito, and passed Gerónimo, who looked at me in a special way, as if reminding me that the devils were running loose. We went up to my mother's room, saw her lying in bed, and understood that she had died so filled with pain there was no room for the final, physical pain the pills might have caused her. Braulia had already cleaned her face, which was serene. I stood looking closely at her. I didn't dare touch her; I saw an abyss and at the same time a boundary. A repose that was hers and mine. Papá told me to kiss her, and I leaned over the bed to do it; first I kissed her forehead, icy and with the same apple smell that had enveloped me when I came in. Then I kissed her hand, and this was a longer kiss, like a phrase I whispered to her. When I looked up I saw the silhouette of J.T. leaning against the doorjamb. I couldn't see his face because the light was shining right at me, but I knew he could see mine perfectly well. I got up to make my escape, and the Captain moved aside to let me pass. I went directly to my room to find my cards; I had an inexplicable impulse to find some cards I'd had for a long time and put them in order, arrange the cards while I sat on the bed, without any purpose, just thinking.

When dusk fell I went into the hall and saw out of the corner of my eye that the door to my mother's room was closed. I went downstairs holding the cards; I did it slowly because I noticed that the furniture in the living room had been moved and some chairs grouped together, all for the wake. The coffin hadn't come yet, but there were flowers and candles, and a strange iron crucifix that looked like a sword. I ran out of there, walked to the hotel, and took refuge in some corner of the entrance to play with my cards again. Then I heard the Captain's footsteps, which were unmistakable. He stopped beside me and tousled my hair—he'd never do that again—and it seemed to me he moved away, but then he stopped, as if expecting me to say something to him. I bit my lips. I wanted to talk and be quiet, I wanted to shout, die, tear the world apart. That was when I heard him say: "This is how you grow, son." J.T. moved slowly toward my house. And a few minutes later I went after him.

*WHAT if I told you that a part of me, just a small part, also needs to know what happened? Hasn't it occurred to you that maybe it's why I made an appointment with you on St. Croix and came all this way, more dead than alive? What I couldn't or didn't want to see for so many years I have to look at now, and every minute until the end, as if you were shoving me into a tunnel with the barrel of a gun at the back of my neck, telling me to look straight ahead and no false moves or I'd be sorry.*

*Your father didn't want anybody to see him in Isabel Segunda. The town was seething after the uprising, and he thought he ought to fall off the map for a few days. On Wednesday, which was November 1, he asked me to take you to school, since they'd sent Gerónimo somewhere with the truck, probably to pick up fish. I took care of giving you a few strict warnings, something your father hadn't done. It was dangerous for you to begin to say that you knew the barber, and especially that you knew Roberto and had seen him at the hotel—you saw him frequently, though you've erased the memory—and that he was a friend of the family, particularly of your mother's. I lied to you. I assured you Frank had told me to tell you to keep your mouth shut, because you wouldn't have wanted to listen to me. You were a bright kid, I didn't have to insist too much.*

*As soon as I dropped you off at school, I went back to Martineau. There are feelings that can be explained only at the end of our days, from the perspective of the blows that bring us down. That morning I could have stayed in Isabel Segunda, walked into some café, and had a couple of beers. Or I could have gone to Mosquito, which was my original plan, and spent the morning checking out one of the Cessna's propellers that was making an annoying noise and had me worried. There were a lot of things I could have done besides going into your house then, with your mother in bed and your father practically in bed too, because he had gone to one of the rooms in the hotel to smoke one cigarette after another and listen to the news on the radio. But Eugene the Jeep, an individual with premonitions, headed straight for Frank's Guesthouse. I almost didn't have to drive it, I felt as if it were moving of its own volition. For a moment the possibility crossed my mind that they had gone to arrest your father, and maybe Estela too. I chased away that idea and used the brake, forced myself to drive more slowly, and as I was coming into Martineau I saw something unreal: a stout old man, his torso bare, hanging a dog. Another dog sat beside him, closely watching the operation. I slowed down, and the old man looked at me. The dog was still kicking its legs in the air as it hung from the rope; it was an enormous animal, and I thought the man must be extraordinarily strong to have held it up. I thought about Rienzi's—see how those hidden memories come back again. I remembered my own anguish when the Greek boy said his line: "But the night is beginning now, and it would be good to obey it." A night was beginning in that place, there where an old lunatic was sacrificing a dog, which was also the place where a man without a compass, watching him from the road, came to understand a subtle horror.*

*I floored the accelerator and almost crashed three or four times before I reached the door of the hotel. I jumped out of the Jeep and ran to your house: everyone was there, including a couple who were staying at the hotel, a couple from Georgia with their little girl, a strange little girl with the face of a goblin. I went up to your mother's room and ran into Braulia, who asked me not to leave Frank's side. "There's nothing anyone can do," she said. "She was alive when I found her. But she's gone, I know she's gone." Your father was sitting on the bed and holding up Estela's corpse by the shoulders, still trying to make her respond. He saw me arrive and asked if the doctor had come. I said no, at least I hadn't seen him. It didn't matter because what I wanted to know was if she was still breathing. I looked for the pulse in her neck; I opened her robe and pressed my ear to her heart; I put a mirror under her nose. Frank murmured: "I did all that. She hasn't breathed for a while." I looked at the mirror and saw that it was true. Estela was dead, her face streaked with vomit. She had taken barbiturates but also had soaked a handkerchief in chloroform, or something like it, and held the handkerchief over her nose. That's how Braulia found her, doubly asleep, and when she tried to shake her to make her respond, your mother gave a kind of sigh that apparently was her last. They called the doctor, who wasn't in Isabel Segunda. Gerónimo had the truck, and your father didn't even remember that he'd asked me to take you to school; he began shouting like a madman that they had to find me and tell me to bring the Jeep. Braulia tried to impose reason: there was nothing to do because Estela was dead. She was trying to convince him of this when she saw me arrive. They traded roles, and now it was your father who tried to convince me because, even after confirming that she wasn't breathing, I insisted we take her in the Jeep and go for help. "There's no point," he said finally, asserting his authority. "It's over, J. T." He stopped holding her up by the shoulders and arranged her on the bed, like a dead person, the way dead people are arranged. I collapsed into a chair and heard your father making a strange noise through his nose, as if he were blowing it a lot of times; it was his way of sobbing. I wanted to tell him that we ought to wait a little, that Estela probably would respond when Braulia forced one of her concoctions on her, but I felt dazed, as if I'd also been put to sleep with chloroform, or whatever the hell it was. I know it was a blue vial with a liquid that smelled like apples. After soaking the handkerchief, your mother let the vial drop to the floor. God only knows how she got it.*

*For a while we didn't say anything, and your father, sobbing in that irritating way, put his arms around Estela's legs. I let him do it because I was remembering the day when I met all of you, first Frank, a young man trying to make a go of his guesthouse, and then you and your mother. You were the little obstacle in the arms of the woman for whose sake I decided to come back, and come back, and spend the years coming back. Braulia interrupted the memory: she brought sponges and tow-*

*els and the two maids to help her clean the room while she tidied your mother. I took Frank by the arm and dragged him to the hotel. We drank a little, we smoked without stopping. Your father kept saying: "I should have known she'd do something like this." I didn't answer because I knew he was right. We both should have known that Estela would do something crazy, which is the easy way to say she'd do exactly what was expected of her: a logical act, thoroughly thought out and planned according to the outcome of the uprising. She'd hoarded the barbiturates for months, ever since her visit to the doctor in San Juan, which is when she must have gotten the vial of chloroform too.*

*It was close to midday when they told us the doctor had come. I didn't go back to the house with your father; I didn't want to be present for those formalities. I suspected that the punctilious doctor—a fat little man with gray sideburns who wore a cap that looked more like a kepi than a cap—would listen to Estela's heart and palpate her belly, and I was sure he'd finish up by opening her eyes and shining a light to see inside them. The last thing I wanted to see was your mother's green eyes and the color they'd taken on at the moment of death, turned toward the verge of indifference. I stayed in the hotel; I was sleepy, or thought I was. An hour went by, maybe more; I think I fell asleep in one of the chairs in the lobby, or I passed out.*

*The next thing I saw was Gerónimo's face, he used to call me Captain too, except he'd say it in English, and it sounded something like "Coptén," said in a leaden voice. I opened my eyes, and he gave a jump, startled to see in my eyes the image of the swamp where I'd been slogging. From a wary distance, he asked if he ought to go for the boy. The boy was you, naturally, left on your own when you got out of school. I shook my head and looked at the time. I said that in my state I couldn't drive, and if he wanted to he could take the Jeep. Gerónimo was a colorless creature. "I'd better go in the truck," he mumbled. I went up to my room and washed my face. I looked at myself in the mirror, and kept looking at myself as I emitted a few sobs similar to your father's, as nasal and annoying as Frank's. Perhaps some men don't know how to cry any other way. What had ended for me was not only a woman but a place,*

*a period, some plans for my life. Now it didn't matter anymore if the
plans were fantastic. While the illusion lasted, I could keep myself ac-
tive, traveling from one island to another, carrying merchandise or dead
people; I'd happily carried my corpses, some more rigid, others less.
Sometimes I heard them talking.*

*I poured another drink. My head was foggy, but I was still sober
enough to worry about what Gerónimo would say to you. I knew that
as soon as you saw him you'd know something serious had happened.
Gerónimo, besides being colorless, was unpredictable, a very strange creature. That was why I believed him capable of telling you your father
hadn't come for you and neither had I because we were busy with your
dead mother. Said that way, coming raw out of the swampland of his
voice, the news would crush you. You'd be crushed when you got to Martineau, and you'd look for your father right away. I decided I wouldn't
be present then either. I saw the truck arrive, saw you make a dash for
the house, closely followed by Gerónimo. A short time later you came out
with Frank, and the two of you began to walk toward the beach. I imagined you were going to talk.*

*After a while, and two or three generous drinks, I felt ready to go
back to the house. I wanted to see Estela and say goodbye to her from my
fog, without hope. But I couldn't because you and your father had come
back, and just as I started to go into her room I saw you kissing her; you
kissed her on the forehead, or on the lips, and then you kissed her hands.
Light was coming in from the hall and shining in your face, and it was
your face, they way you narrowed your eyes to see who the intruder was,
that filled me with a kind of clairvoyance. I suddenly intuited that nothing was left in the room. Not only was Estela not there but you weren't
either, or your father, who had been my friend. I didn't even feel capable
of making certain I was who I was. The death in the room was a broth
that transformed us into strange beings, into macabre shreds of people,
vestiges of unrecognizable animals.*

*You got up to leave, and I moved away from the door. I thought I'd
never spend another minute alone with your father. Not a single one. I
think you went into your room, and I took the Jeep and drove to Mos-*

quito. I had to check the propeller; it made a noise that worried me. But I took off without looking at it. I felt relieved when I did that; I climbed easily and no sound disturbed me. The Parakeet Cessna was flying as usual, except that somebody else was piloting it. In the air I howled, I shouted where no one could hear me, I turned at La Esperanza to do a somersault I'd seen my father do many years earlier. I knew I wouldn't do it well; the plane could fall in a spiral and I wouldn't be able to regain control. Then I didn't have the balls; I couldn't do the somersault or simply crash the plane. It's a great fallacy that suicides are the most desperate people. There's a scale to desperation: when you reach a certain point, you can do it. Past that point, wounded to your very soul, you can't even end it with dignity. I returned to Mosquito in an absolute downpour and skidded when I landed. The inside of the Cessna smelled of vomit because I vomited when I made the turn at La Esperanza; my mouth tasted bitter, and I felt a vast disgust with myself and everything around me. I remembered that in the rear of the plane, in the toolbox, I had a bottle of rum that was half-full. I hurried to find it and drank eagerly, standing motionless in the rain, looking at Eugene the Jeep on the other side of the runway, its silhouette blurred and ironic at the same time. I tossed the bottle on the ground, next to the plane, and decided not to stay for the funeral.

I went to Martineau to pick up my things, my valise filled with papers, my clothes, some flight maps, everything I had left in the room. I wanted to tell your father I couldn't stay but would help him any way I could if he needed me to take care of anything in Isabel Segunda. When I passed the hotel on my way to the house, I saw you sitting on the ground, playing with some cards, pretending you were playing, in reality you were devastated, dirty, your face covered with snot. You looked up; you had so much rage in your body you reminded me of one of those retarded children, pop-eyed and with a stupid mouth hanging open, drooling. I remember I kept walking, but then I thought better of it and stopped; I said something about blows making us grow, or some asinine remark like that. In any case, you went on looking at me with rage, and I acknowledged receipt of the blow.

*I went straight to your mother's room. I supposed that Frank would be with her, or Braulia. I'd looked for Braulia in the kitchen, but the house seemed deserted. I pushed the door to the room, which was not completely closed, and I saw the profile that moved me so. I've already told you that the voice is the last thing to go, that whispers and occasional words float in the air for several hours over lifeless bodies. I've confirmed this with all the corpses I carried in the plane. And I could confirm it with Estela. I went into the room and closed the door. I was dripping wet, and I took off my shoes. Even at a moment as devastating as that, all I could think of was the hard time Braulia would give me when she saw the floor covered with puddles. Then I approached the bed. Your mother was clean and combed, covered to the neck with a linen sheet. Beside her, in the spot where I suspect your father slept, there was a gray dress that was too severe, which I supposed was the one they'd put on her for the coffin. When I leaned over to look at the dress, a few drops of water fell from my head. I looked around for a towel or a cloth but didn't find one. I took off my shirt and tried to dry my hair with it, but at the same time I lifted the sheet to keep the water from soaking through to Estela's skin. She was naked, perfumed and dry, totally dry, and I'd bet not as cold as and much less rigid than anyone would have suspected.*

*I sat beside her on the edge of the bed and lifted her hands, which Braulia had folded on her chest. I leaned over to kiss her fingers, and after I kissed them her hands unfolded; it was a magical gesture that revealed her nipples. I was invaded by sorrow and a lack of control that made me ashamed. With great shame I pressed my face to her flesh and moved up, sniffing at her, searching for an odor I could renounce later. Suddenly I found myself lying beside her, literally embracing her body, and I realized that my trousers, dirty with the dust of the runway at Mosquito and befouled by vomit, could soil the sheets and your mother's skin, ruining Braulia's superb work, which had left her unblemished. I stood up and took them off. I tossed them away and returned to Estela. I buried my face in her hair and I was floating, feeling myself overcome by drowsiness, the weariness that had pursued me since midday, a drunkenness different from real drunkenness but also combined with it.*

*I was half-asleep as I searched for her lips, which were partially open. With no disgust, with love and naturalness, I put my tongue between them, and only in that instant did I touch the ice, the stupor of nothingness, a viscous enigma that was her tongue at rest. I moved my face away with a brusque movement and let it fall on her chest, sobbing the way your father did, as if I were blowing my nose, my entire body shaking, dying of cold and remorse.*

# CHAPTER ELEVEN

BRAULIA wasn't in the house and neither was Papá. They'd both left in the truck, I think to buy a coffin and notify people in Isabel Segunda. After mussing my hair and making some drunken remark, J.T. entered the house and went into the kitchen. He called for Braulia, and in the silence of midafternoon, those shouts of his seemed like an insult. I slipped into the dining room and crouched behind the table, and from there I saw him head for the steps and stagger upstairs. I intuited that the Captain's only destination was my mother's room, that he was going there; I seemed to guess he'd stop in front of the door, breathing hard, gathering strength, and then kick it open, like a cowboy sowing panic in a bar. From my hiding place I could tell my intuition was correct: I heard the noise of its rebound against the wall, and then the other noise when the door was closed. It was a dry sound that reverberated in my lungs: the Captain was alone with my mother.

I pulled out a chair and sat at the table. If J.T. suddenly opened the door and came down with Mamá in his arms, what could I do to stop him from putting her in the Jeep, driving her to the airstrip at Mosquito, and taking off with her in the plane? Accustomed as he was to flying with cadavers and transporting them from one island to the next, how could he not want to fly one last time with Estela, silent and perfumed, almost awake after Braulia had put creams on her face and cleaned her teeth?

I left the dining room and walked to the staircase. Just the day before, Mamá had been there, curled up on the bottom steps, listening to the voice on the radio telling about the siege at the barbershop. I went up, afraid I'd come face-to-face with the Captain, walking on tiptoe so as not to make noise. I waited outside the door, listening to emptiness, the hum of absolute silence: not a word, not a touch, not the slightest murmur. I opened the door slowly, so quietly and efficiently that for a moment I felt invisible. Braulia had closed the curtains, and it was hard for me to begin defining the shapes. The Captain was standing, without his shirt, leaning over my mother's dead body. His shoes were near the door, and I saw them clearly; there was something sad and repulsive in the untied laces. It was difficult to make out his movements, but I realized he had stood and was trying to undo the button at his waist, until he succeeded and his trousers dropped, wrapped like a cat around his ankles. First J.T. pulled out one foot, and he seemed to sway for a few seconds—it was probably the effect of the alcohol—and then he pulled out the other. Finally he kicked the trousers, and they flew into a corner of the room. He was rigid and naked. At my age, I couldn't imagine how piercing desire can become in a young man full of strength and vitality, branded by disdain and the agony of flying alone, day after day, drunk and carrying excess cargo. The sight of his profile made me sick. Each cell of my body was flooded with disgust, a human disgust that struggled in my head and stomach but couldn't control my blood. My blood went in another direction, carrying a substance I can't name, a sick enthusiasm. The Captain moved toward my mother's dead body, which I saw more and more clearly as my eyes finally became accustomed to the semidarkness. Mamá's body, completely naked, was hidden under the body of J.T., under his shiny back and freckled ass, totally unreal. From the doorway I heard him sniffing and snorting, moaning meekly, stammering a phrase, or spitting, perhaps he was only spitting. Then he leaned on his left arm and raised himself a little, and with his right arm I saw him adjusting my mother's torso, placing it where he wanted it. It seemed he bent one of his knees to separate her legs, and my eyes misted over. The mud in my stomach tightened, and the Captain slipped into horror, into his and into mine, fierce and damned as only a man of his bulk could sink.

I don't know how long it lasted. I can't say either just when J.T. became aware of my presence. I suppose I made a sound, or took an abrupt mouthful of air, like someone who has been submerged for a long time and reaches the surface at the moment of agony. He turned his head, and our glances crossed. It wasn't that we looked into each other's eyes, because that was almost impossible in the semidarkness; it was something monstrous, much more intense. Neither of us could come back from the frontier; there was no return and we both knew it. I ran down the stairs, left the house in terror, and barely had time to reach the courtyard: I began to vomit at the same instant and didn't stop until they took me out of Martineau and gave me shots of sedatives so that I'd sleep, so that when I woke again I wouldn't see anything but the imaginary lights I'd been talking to for several months. The Captain got up and put on his wet clothing. He covered my mother again, made an effort to leave everything just as he'd found it. Braulia, who had washed her, and my father, tormented by the stupid question of the coffin— he was obsessed for several days by the idea that he hadn't been able to find a single deluxe coffin in Isabel Segunda—never discovered that Mamá's body had been profaned. They both died not knowing it.

J.T. picked up his things, and the Parakeet Cessna took off for the last time from the airstrip that for so many years had seen him arrive, drop off the cargo, and leave with different cargo, or with some paying passenger, or with us, his friends from Frank's Guesthouse, the members of the Yasín family. For a few months my aunt looked after me. She visited me every day in the hospi-

tal in San Juan, and then took me to her house until I'd recovered enough to return to Vieques. But when I arrived in Martineau, everybody thought they'd put another boy in my place.
Braulia had already left the hotel and was living with Gertrudis,
on the same coffee plantation where she ended her days, thirty-
five years later, when she was almost ninety. Papá had two buy-
ers for the hotel, but neither was prepared to pay him even half
of what he assured them the land and the two structures, the
hotel and the house, were worth. We still had one more summer left, the summer of 1951. Gerónimo was with us, and
Elodio Brito was still cooking, but it was clear that the soul of
Martineau—my mother—as well as the brains and in a sense the
muscle—Braulia—were missing. The Captain was missing too;
he never returned to his room. Other guests stayed in it, and by
then I had torn up the photograph in which he appears in profile, leaning against the plane, looking toward the La Esperanza
reefs. I destroyed it, swearing I'd kill him wherever I happened
to see him again.

In time we moved to San Juan. I lived with my aunt while
my father tried his luck in the United States, first in Florida and
then in Georgia, where he already had some friends. Among
those friends was the couple who'd stayed at the hotel at the
time my mother died. They had a little girl who cried too
much, a confused little girl with blond hair who wanted them
to hold her all the time. The man died, and the widow continued her correspondence with Papá until finally they met and
decided to marry. I was present at their wedding. Helen confessed to me that on the very day my mother died, she dreamed
she was married to the owner of the hotel. The dream seemed
like nonsense to her, but later she understood that sleepers, at
a desolate point in the night, cross paths in their flight with
the dead. She spoke to me that way, and I felt it in my bones. I
felt cold, and I felt compassion. I particularly felt nostalgia. We
were in Georgia, and it was autumn, but even there the smell of

jellyfish rotting on the shore reached me, the same sharp smell we breathed in on the balconies of our hotel whenever October approached. In winter only a trace of the chain of dried jellyfish remained on the sand: a soft green thread that was both grief and a tireless enigma.

"I won't see this place again," the Captain declared. "That's a relief."

I picked him up at the hospital and we shared a taxi to the airport. At his request, the driver took an unnecessary turn around Christiansted, but the Captain didn't even bother to take a last look at the streets. He said what he said with his eyes fastened on his hands, which he rested on his knees, as if he could contemplate the original landscape there: the one from the years when we would come to the Pink Fancy and visit the port in the morning, and on some afternoons take long excursions that almost always ended at the yellow tower of Fort Christiansvaern, where an old woman would sit and sell *maubi*, my mother's favorite drink, and another old woman sold us titty bread, a loaf with two peaks that I loved.

"One morning a few months ago," the Captain murmured, "when they were giving me the chemo injection, I thought I'd lose my hair, all my hair and my eyebrows. Can you believe that at those moments I thought about the barber?"

I said nothing. He thought I didn't know which barber he was referring to.

"The day they killed him," he added in a whisper, "was the last time I saw your mother alive."

"They didn't kill him," I revealed angrily, as if he'd said

something offensive. "They gave him the coup de grâce, but he survived."

The Captain passed his tongue over his lips. I was about to ask him if he wanted to stop the cab and buy a bottle of water. I thought better of it before I opened my mouth.

"He survived? Somebody told me he died. It must have been your father who wrote about it in a letter to me."

I shook my head. I said that when the police finally got inside the barbershop, they found Vidal unconscious, lying in a puddle of blood. A sergeant who was leading the assault group shot him in the head. The bullet lodged in his skull, in a delicate spot, and I don't believe they ever could extract it. He spent weeks in the hospital, dying on some days, recovering on others. After two months, the doctors decided he was out of danger and could go to prison. That's how he began serving his sentence, like a poor, patched ghost. He had a purple hole on his forehead, the mark of the coup de grâce, and a useless, or almost useless hand full of scars and missing a couple of fingers. He had to learn to hold the scissors with his good hand, and common criminals offered their heads for Vidal to practice on. They weren't the great heads of the revolution he had trimmed in the old days but living hair that he cut with pleasure and that helped him recover his skill. He left prison years later, transformed into a new barber with another kind of hand and another kind of glance. My father didn't see him again. He had sent him some help with the nationalists who came to visit him and his wife, and he told me in a letter that he heard Vidal was working again, as it happened in the barbershop of a hotel, which surely would make him think about the summer of 1950, when he gave haircuts to all the guests in Frank's Guesthouse.

"All of them except me," the Captain said. "I was afraid of his scissors. That barber looked at me in a strange way. In any case, I was a gringo and couldn't take the chance."

We arrived at the airport. An employee of the airline came

toward us, pushing the wheelchair the hospital had requested. He signaled to J.T., who hesitated before sitting down; I imagined it repelled him and, down deep, embarrassed him. Then he gave in, looking into my eyes; it was a look filled with pity—pity for me, I felt it in my bones—and I held his glance as long as I could.

"And you," he said, refusing to change the subject, "didn't you see him again either?"

I hesitated for a few seconds. It seemed to me that I had, I had seen him again. It happened on a day when I was walking down Calle Cuevillas toward a restaurant where Gladys was waiting for me. I noticed that a man standing in the doorway of a barbershop was looking at me. I'd just come back from Vietnam and was conscious of people looking at lame young men. But the man's stare bothered me, and I thought about saying something nasty to him. I was just about to when I realized he was the barber. "But you're Vidal!" I exclaimed. He nodded with a smile, and the purple scar on his forehead turned a deeper purple. "I'm Andrés Yasín, don't you remember me?" He took a step back and concentrated on my face. "We said goodbye in 1949 at my father's hotel." I saw his expression change suddenly; a violent shadow divided his face. "My mother asked you to cut my hair, and you gave me a cadet's beret." The barber stammered an excuse. "Her name was Estela. We lived in Martineau." He retreated into the barbershop, and the scar on his forehead turned into an eye. "No, I don't remember." His mouth was quivering, he began to perspire, and he turned his back on me.

"A coup de grâce," the Captain murmured sadly, "is what some of us need."

At that moment they announced his flight. The Captain blinked several times, and I believe he did it intentionally, with rigor and malice, as if he were warning me of a danger.

"The turtles," he said at last, and I discovered that he was casting an uncertain line as leathery as eels. "Don't you remember that guy on Buck Island who sold stuffed turtles?"

Sammy. The guy who sold them was named Sammy, a skinny black with a rotting nose. He put live turtles next to stuffed ones and dying ones in order to fool his customers.

"He stuffed them very badly," the Captain said. "They stank like hell. I once gave one to Estela, and you insisted on keeping it. You wanted it for your very own, you said, and you kept pleading, demanding that she give it to you until she gave in—that's what a mother does, isn't it? But in a few days the turtle started to rot in your room; it turned into carrion, and the stink was enough to kill you. You don't know how happy that made me, fucking demanding brat."

He swallowed, and something comical rose and fell along his skinny neck, crisscrossed with veins.

"The fact is you were afraid. Fear deceived you, and you've gone on being deceived all these years. When I went to say goodbye to your mother, it was growing dark. It got dark very quickly. How could you see what you say you saw? Think, damn it, just ask yourself this question: what else did you want for your very own?"

My shoulders hunched, I felt a deadly pain in the back of my neck. The airline employee came over then to tell him they were about to board. He went behind the wheelchair and signaled to me that he was about to take him away.

"I'm going," I said to him.

"Stay," J.T. ordered. It was the first time in all those days that his voice reminded me of the real voice of the Captain of the Sleepers. "We'll say goodbye."

He held out his hand, which was cold, and I shook it with my own hand, old and icy.

"Clear this up for me," he insisted, not letting me go. "You wanted it all, didn't you?"

The employee began to push him toward the boarding gate. Before they went through I saw J.T. give me a look free of sadness or irony, a totally young look. I must have seemed like an imaginary child to him, a depraved insomniac. He raised his voice so that I could hear him clearly:

"Sweet dreams, Andrés. Sleep tight!"

A NOTE ABOUT THE AUTHOR

Mayra Montero is the author of a collection of short stories and of seven novels, most of which have been translated into English by Edith Grossman. She was born in Cuba and lives in Puerto Rico, where she writes a weekly column in *El Nuevo Día* newspaper.


A NOTE ABOUT THE TRANSLATOR

Edith Grossman is the award-winning translator of works by major Spanish-language authors, including Gabriel García Márquez, Álvaro Mutis, Mario Vargas Llosa, Julián Ríos, and Miguel de Cervantes, as well as Mayra Montero. She lives in New York.